Catharine McKenty's combination of meticulous research, imaginative engagement with her subject, and flair for narrative has resulted in a story that captures two historical worlds, Ireland and Canada in the ninetenth-century, so that her heroine, Mary Ann Noble, is brought to life in ways that not only illustrate her exceptional personality but evoke aspects of history that can be instructive for our time.

Dr Michael Kenneally
Principal, Concordia University School of Canadian Irish Studies
Honorary Consul General of Ireland

The author sets a marvellous example of how to go about doing research at the local level, talking to people on the ground, assembling as much surviving historical evidence as possible, and presenting it in a most engaging way. I do hope that it may be possible for the Centre for Migration Studies to help facilitate the development of links between schools in Ireland and Canada. I do hope that local schools (and not only local schools) will take up the offer that the book presents to them.

Brian Lambkin
Director, Centre for Migration Studies, Ulster American Folk Park
Castleton, Omagh, Co. Tyrone, Northern Ireland

What a splendid book ... what a delightful story. The bibliography and illustrations give it the right air of authenticity. The book is very educational — all those who read it will hardly notice they are being taught ... the author is a superb storyteller! I could feel the slushy peat field ... I could smell the rain coming.

Marianna O'Gallagher,
Authority on Grosse Île and its preservation as an Irish monument
Quebec City, Canada

Definitely a book for our times, for all age groups. There are hints of the innocence of Anne of Green Gables in this poignant story.

A wonderful, gentle book about a painful time in Irish history. An ageless story of famine amidst plenty, but without bitterness or prejudice.

The publication is also extraordinary in its paper quality, archival photos, illustrations and binding. It would make a great addition to the libraries of schools in Ireland.

Barbara Canella (nee Ennis)
Tyrone Constitution

The story allows complete strangers to connect with the voices of their own past ... we are treated to a vividly imagined Irish childhood of the early nineteenth-century, replete with youthful misadventure, natural disasters, family power struggles, religious tension, and farming.

This book is a swift and pleasant read, the prose at once lyrical and accessible, the pages rife with illustrations, photographs and maps.

A journey immensely worth undertaking.

Alice Abracen
Dawson College Liberal Arts Graduate / Harvard University Freshman
Senior Times

Catharine McKenty draws on a wide range of contemporary sources as she convincingly recreates the life of the rural parish of Dromore and its relationship with the wider world of Omagh, Ireland and the land beyond the Atlantic. This fusion of ancestral study and sheer good story-telling gives us a quite unique publication ... the illustrations can only be described as delightful.

Pat McDonnell
Omagh District Councillor
Ulster Herald

POLLY
OF BRIDGEWATER FARM

AN UNKNOWN IRISH STORY

CATHARINE FLEMING MCKENTY

Third edition 2013

Polly of Bridgewater Farm: An Unknown Irish Story

First published in Canada 2009 by Cabbagetown Press, Toronto, Ontario

Third edition 2013
Copyright © 2013, by Catharine Fleming McKenty
Published by Torchflame Books an imprint of Light Messages Publishing
Printed in the United States of America
ISBN 978-1-61153-066-7

Illustrations, Cover Design, Layout and Text Design:
   Elizabeth Malara-Wieczorek, Darek Wieczorek; http://www.del-art.ca

This edition of *Polly of Bridgewater Farm: An Unknown Irish Story* is based largely
on the first edition published in 2009 by the Cabbagetown Press, the publishing
arm of the Cabbagetown Regent Park Community Museum in Toronto.

Museum Founder and Chair, Carol Moore-Ede, deserves special notice. She
devoted hundreds of hours to the project, including reviewing and copy-editing
the manuscript; selecting and working with the illustrators and book designer;
preparing publishable archival images; and monitoring the printing process.
The text is a slightly revised version of the first edition text. A few new illustrations have been added. The Cabbagetown Press has authorized the reproduction
of the original drawings prepared for the book.

Permissions:
   Annesley Malley, Ireland   Florence Corey
   Barbara Fleming   McCord Museum
   Catharine Fleming McKenty   Royal Ontario Museum
   City of Toronto Archives   Toronto Public Library
   David Clark / Carol Moore-Ede

Torchflame Books
An imprint of Light Messages

For all those who have Irish roots
past, present and future;
and all those
who search for a connection to their own
family story.

Table of Contents

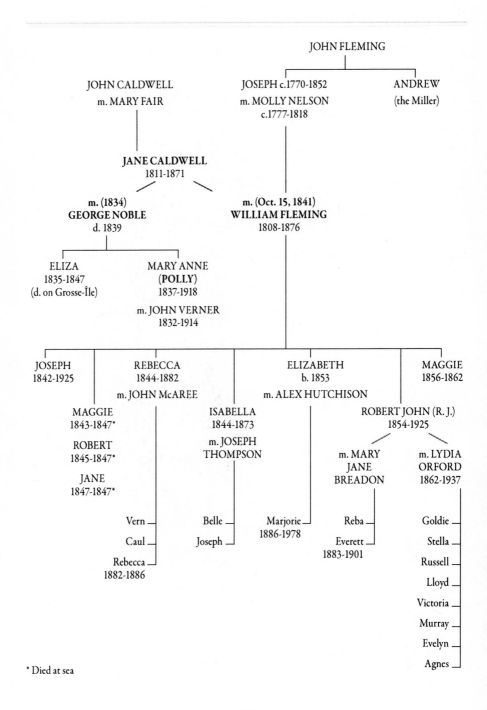

JOHN FLEMING

JOHN CALDWELL
m. MARY FAIR

JOSEPH c.1770-1852
m. MOLLY NELSON
c.1777-1818

ANDREW
(the Miller)

JANE CALDWELL
1811-1871

m. (1834)
GEORGE NOBLE
d. 1839

m. (Oct. 15, 1841)
WILLIAM FLEMING
1808-1876

ELIZA
1835-1847
(d. on Grosse-Île)

MARY ANNE
(POLLY)
1837-1918
m. JOHN VERNER
1832-1914

JOSEPH
1842-1925

REBECCA
1844-1882
m. JOHN McAREE

ELIZABETH
b. 1853
m. ALEX HUTCHISON

MAGGIE
1856-1862

MAGGIE
1843-1847*

ROBERT
1845-1847*

JANE
1847-1847*

ISABELLA
1844-1873
m. JOSEPH
THOMPSON

ROBERT JOHN (R. J.)
1854-1925

m. MARY
JANE
BREADON

m. LYDIA
ORFORD
1862-1937

Vern

Caul

Rebecca
1882-1886

Belle

Joseph

Marjorie
1886-1978

Reba

Everett
1883-1901

Goldie

Stella

Russell

Lloyd

Victoria

Murray

Evelyn

Agnes

* Died at sea

8

Mary Anne Noble Verner
(Polly).

Joseph Fleming; older brother of R. J. Fleming
Mid August, 1842- January 16, 1925.

Arrival in Toronto.

Notice to passengers of the ship, Superior, *in port and bound for Quebec, Canada.*

DANIEL BAIRD & Co., Who will dispose of the Cargo of the above Ship, on arrival, consisting of INDIAN CORN, FLOUR, &c., &c., on reasonable terms,

Londonderry, 1st May, 1847.

NOW IN PORT

NOTICE TO PASSENGERS.

 Those Persons who have taken their Passages by the Ship

SESOSTRIS,

Captain DANT.

FOR QUEBEC.

ARE required to be in Derry on TUESDAY, the 17th MAY, pay the remainder of their Passage Money and go on Board, as the Vessel will go to sea immediately after that date.

Londonderry, May 4, 1847.   **J. & J. COOKE.**

The Ship PORTLAND Captain STALKER, for ST. JOHN'S, about the 20th MAY.

NOW IN PORT—NOTICE TO PASSENGERS

Notice to passengers of the ship, Sesostris, *in port and bound for Quebec, Canada.*

Mary Anne Noble Verner
'Aunt Polly' (1837-1918).

John Verner
(1832-1914).

Sketch of the Cabbagetown Store.

Acknowledgements

With heartfelt thanks to:

Florence and Seamus Corey and their family who have welcomed me home every year since 2002 with family events, good food, a roof over my head, and their knowledge of the old ways;

Robert Funston, Pat McDonnell, Eveline and Ynr Smith, Ashley and Jane Patterson, the McNabb family, Valerie Jackson, Burt Duncan, Madge Cunningham, who shared in the welcome, with evenings of music, story-telling, excursions, and a book launch that raised money for clean water and a school in Africa;

*Breege McCusker who made Polly's story part of her 2002 Christmas broadcast on **BBC Northern Ireland**, and Gerry Cooley of Dublin Nearfm. Wesley Atcheson, editor of the **Tyrone Constitution**, who introduced Polly to his readers, followed by the Ulster Herald;*

Dr. Patrick Fitzgerald, Liam Corey, Brian Lambkin at the Ulster American Folk Park; Mickey McGuinness, and Annesley Malley, who shared a lifetime's knowledge of sailing ships; John Cunningham, Dr Haldane Mitchell, Steve McKenna, and the staff of the Omagh Public Library.

*Our much missed Marianna O'Gallagher (Grosse-Île) and Professor Clare Maloney who shared their expertise; John Griffin, descendant of Brian Boru, who launched the haunting melody **Polly of Bridgewater Farm** at my 80th birthday party in Dromore with Scott and Kate Griffin; John Perry who gave me a Montreal diary; John Fleming for his help with this edition, all the Fleming relatives for their support, and my husband Neil McKenty who shared this incredible journey with laughter and patience.*

*Special thanks indeed to Carol Moore-Ede, Executive Producer, Director, Writer for CBC-TV 1969-2009; Founder and Chair of the **Cabbagetown Regent Park Museum, Toronto**, who put all her expertise into the production of this book (see credit page for details), met impossible deadlines, encouraged me every step of the way along with a dedicated team of museum volunteers, and then defied the Icelandic volcano to ship 500 books across the Atlantic for schools in Northern Ireland;*

Marion Blake, Cynthia Macdonald, Gail Mostyn, and Richard Stanley Rice, an indomitable team.

Darek and Elizabeth Wieczorek, who had their own publishing house in Poland and brought their unique artistry to these pages.

The contribution of each person mentioned above to "Polly of Bridgewater Farm" is immeasurable. In a very real sense this book is an on-going community effort.

Catharine Fleming McKenty

"There may be many a land where the verdure blooms more in fragrance and in richness — where the clime breathes softer, and a brighter sky lights up the landscape, but there is none ... where more touching and heart-bound associations are blended with the features of the soil than in Ireland, and cold must be the spirit, and barren the affections of him who can dwell amidst its mountains and its valleys, its tranquil lakes, its wooded fens, without feeling their humanizing influence upon him."

"Charles O'Malley, the Irish Dragoon"
by Charles Lever
1841

Painting of Derry Harbour, 1840s.

PROLOGUE

Polly Noble was born in 1837 on a farm near the old coach road from Dromore to Enniskillen. Dromore was then a tiny village of two streets nestled among the ancient drumlin hills of County Tyrone in Ulster, about nine miles from Omagh.

Polly and her family left Ireland 10 years later in the midst of the Great Famine and settled first in Montreal, Quebec, Canada.

On the evening of April 25, 1849, 12-year-old Polly and her companion John Verner, five years older, were visiting Montreal's colourful Bonsecours market. She had a mop of unruly dark brown hair, a firm chin and clear grey-green eyes that had already seen too much for such a young person. John had come with his family from Ulster in 1840 and apprenticed as a tailor. His family and their neighbours the Breadons had been kindness itself to Polly and her family.

Young John was determined to show Polly all the sights of her new home. In winter they met to view the spectacular ice-palace glistening in the sun at Fletcher's Field. On this particular day, they were exploring the vast port with sailing ships coming in from all over the world.

Suddenly they heard shouts of "Fire, fire!" and saw people running along the cobbled streets in the direction of Parliament Square. As Polly and John followed, they saw flames shooting up from the roof and walls of the stately St. Anne's Market that had served as Parliament House of the United Province of Canada for the last five years. The unruly mob, which had caused the fire, were still shouting in the square, unaware that in their fury at the passage

The Burning of the Parliament Building in Montreal.

of the Rebellion Losses Bill and at a colonial government in general, these normally respectable citizens had just succeeded in depriving Montreal of its vocation as a capital city.

"What a silly thing to do," Polly murmured, and John was relieved to see the colour coming back to her cheeks. Polly would long remember this evening, not just because of the fire, but because then and there she decided this kind young man was the one she was going to marry.

In 1850, Polly and her family left Montreal and moved to Toronto. At 17, she married John Verner and soon they opened a small grocery store in Cabbagetown in downtown Toronto at 283 Parliament street. It offered credit to families a week away from insolvency. One after another a dozen children who had lost their mothers landed on their doorstep. This book is the Irish part of her story that none of these children knew.

Little did Polly realise then that their grocery store in Cabbagetown would become famous to thousands of Canadians across the country through the newspaper columns of Vern McAree, a writer for *The Mail and Empire*[1] and *The Globe and Mail*, or that she would be the heroine of his classic **Cabbagetown Store**[2]. Vern was among those dozen children who had lost their mothers, mainly in childbirth, who came to live at the store.

---

[1] *It had the largest morning circulation — more than any two others — and the sixth largest in North America. It later merged with* The Globe *to become* The Globe and Mail

[2] *"Cabbagetown Store" now available on the Cabbagetown Regent Park Museum website: www.crpmuseum.com*

Author's Note:

My grandfather, Robert John Fleming, was another of those children. He was Aunt Polly's younger step-brother. He came to live with her and Uncle John when he was seventeen, after the death of their mother. Later he became four-time mayor of Toronto. Neither he nor any of us knew the Irish part of the family story, and yet in moments of crisis I felt I could reach back into Aunt Polly's strength, even though I had never met her.

R. J. and Lydia Fleming at their marriage.

When I was growing up, few people talked about the million people who died of hunger and disease in the Great Famine.

In 2002, thanks to Robert Funston, and Florence and Seamus Corey, I set foot at long last on the Fleming farm, on the old coach road near Dromore, nine miles from Omagh in Co. Tyrone, Northern Ireland. To my amazement the old whitewashed stone house was still there. As I was leaving the farm, walking alone down the lane, I heard voices talking. It was suddenly clear to me that these were voices from the past, as though an invisible curtain had been pulled aside for a brief moment. I had to find out what these voices were saying. This book is the result. It begins two years before Polly's birth in 1835 when a young ordnance surveyor sets out from Dublin to find Dromore just as I did.

The old coach road leading to Bridgewater Farm.

Spillar's Place, Omagh.

CHAPTER I

Dublin, 1835

A wet and windy day early in November.

Edgar Plimsoll, civil servant, sat fuming in his office at the back of Mountjoy House, headquarters of the famed Ordnance Survey at Phoenix Park. He was struggling manfully to find something at the bottom of an enormous pile of maps, drawings and reports on the desk in front of him.

"Willy!" he bellowed. "Willy, where the devil is that report on Dromore? It was due days ago. Heads will roll if we don't get this mess off our hands soon."

"I did Dromore like you said," muttered Willoughby, a lanky youth of indefinite age, who detested his nickname. "It's in here somewhere." He pulled at a corner of the pile and the whole heap slid gracefully and inexorably to the floor.

"There are two Dromores, you idiot," snapped Plimsoll, as he struggled to disentangle the heap, "and the one you can hardly find on the map is missing. Without it, we can't hand in Tyrone. Why we bother I sometimes wonder. This whole ordnance survey has gotten out of hand if you ask me." No one had in fact asked his opinion, but that never stopped Edgar. He actually liked this brightest of his new recruits, foresaw a fine career ahead of him, but he was stubborn, needed a good push now and then, like all the Welsh.

"You'd better get to it. Take the mail coach tonight to Omagh. Stop at the Royal Arms Hotel. They say it's one of the best in the county. Orr, the owner, will give you a good horse there. And look sharp. The Duke of Wellington is expecting results for all this money Treasury is spending. Though why he thinks anyone can organize the Irish is beyond me, and himself an Irishman."

Willy left in a huff. His grandfather was Irish and he was tired of hearing these constant caricatures. By the time he arrived at Gosson's Hotel in Bolton Street, there were no inside seats left. Thus at 7:30 that night, he found himself perched precariously on top of the lurching coach, as the horses galloped down the darkening roads. He remembered all the lurid tales of highwaymen he had heard from colleagues, especially John O'Donovan, their place name and Irish language expert. One time O'Donovan had taken the night coach from Londonderry to Omagh. It set off with eighteen passengers clinging for dear life outside, and ten passengers crammed inside, himself clutching his umbrella as a shelter from the driving rain and wind, his feet almost frozen from the cold. As if this wasn't enough, didn't the coach overturn in the mud just past Strabane.

"When in doubt, walk, my boy," advised O'Donovan. He himself had done just that, only to discover next morning that the coach for Dublin had departed without him. And to add insult to injury his superior, Larcom, had warned him solemnly to omit all 'ribaldry' in his survey reports. To which he is said to have agreed to make all his future communications "very serious, cold and un-Irish.'"

Hours later, Willy arrived in Omagh, sleepless, soaked to the skin, and with a cold well on its way. If only he could have stayed put for a day or two at the comfortable inn where a hot meal was set down before him.

The next morning a stable lad provided Willy with "one of his best horses." No sign of Mr. Orr, the owner, who was "away on business." It was still pouring rain when master and beast, both equally disgruntled, plodded along the muddy road in the direction of Dromore. Halfway there the horse stumbled and threw a shoe, in sheer spite, Willy declared later.

Willoughby George Hemans arrives at his destination.

A bedraggled figure stood hesitantly at the open door of Dromore's forge. He was warmly welcomed by the group of men near the blazing fire, who of course wanted to know every detail of his errand, and as much of his life history as he would reveal. He had suddenly become a more interesting person than he had ever thought himself to be. In turn, he was more than a little surprised to discover that even the poorest labourer in this group had a vocabulary at least three times as large as his English counterpart, drawn from his Irish roots.

Remembering his duties, he queried the smith on how many houses there might be in the village. Thomas O'Neill, a giant of a man, roared with laughter. "I've never counted but I can tell you there are nineteen spirits dealers, and Cassidy's is the best of them. For the rest you'll find two grocers, two bakers if you'll be needing a loaf of bread, one butcher, three cobblers, and if you want a place to stay, there's McCann's hotel, for what it's worth. If you're needing a fresh horse, as by the looks of it you do, there's not a single one for hire here, but George Noble's yer man, up on the coach road to Enniskillen."

And so it was that Willy Hemans found himself on the doorstep of the Noble's house on a hill just off what is now called Bridge Road. Jane Noble, a sturdy young woman of medium height, perhaps three years older than himself, stood in the doorway. She took one look at him. Before he could protest, he found himself supplied with dry clothes, albeit a size too small, a hot meal and a bed for the night.

The next morning, Will, for so he was now called, accompanied his host to the barn to find a suitable mount. Five years older than himself and half a head shorter, George Noble strode ahead so fast, talking rapidly all the while, that Will arrived nearly breathless at the barn, where several pairs of brown eyes stared curiously at him.

Indeed he had come to the right place. He couldn't believe his luck. These horses, he soon discovered, were a cross between the sturdy local mares and the same Irish thoroughbreds that both the Duke of Wellington and Napoleon had ridden at the Battle of Waterloo. George's grandfather had acquired one at the end of the war when they were going cheap at the famous Moy horse fair.

George and Jane wouldn't hear of Will going to stay at McCann's. That night around the fire Will discovered that his host's forebears had almost been born on horseback; reivers (or cattle rustlers if you like) living by their wits on the borderland between England and Scotland. They had been shipped out lock, stock and barrel by James VI of Scotland when he became James I of England. He was glad to get rid of the lot of them, and they, in turn, had as little love for the law and authorities as did their new Irish neighbours. The Nobles on the whole were Presbyterians, but George's father John had loaned three horses to John Wesley, the Methodist preacher, when he came through Trillick and Drumquin.

Every morning Will rose early and rode out to measure the height of hills, the length of rivers and the dimensions of any building that could possibly be of interest. In the evenings, neighbours dropped by after milking time, full of stories and information that unfortunately never made it into his report. He was just twenty-one. This was only his second field assignment and he was still a little in awe of the polished British officers who were in charge at Mountjoy House.

After all, who would ever read these reports? Likely these memoirs that had so excited Colby's successor, the debonair young Lieutenant Larcom (now Superintendent in charge of the whole Mountjoy Ordnance Survey Project), would moulder on some back shelf.

And so Willoughby George Hemans relaxed in the warmth of the Nobles' home and mentally consigned his assignment to oblivion. His real dream was to become a famous engineer on one of the new railroads. Railway fever would soon be sweeping Ireland. Every town in Ireland would want to be on a line. And he was in the right place at the right time to be part of the excitement.

Will explores Dromore.

One neighbour who was intrigued by Will's dream and came by often on these November evenings was Joseph Fleming, a master stonemason, who lived with his son, William, on the farm on the opposite side of the coach road.

While George and William talked horses, Will discovered that Joseph had worked on the new portico of the great courthouse in Omagh that Will had seen through the rain. Will was soon

describing the magnificent Roman arches he had admired when he had reluctantly spent two years with his father in Italy. Resentment against his father, a retired sea captain, who had deserted his mother and five small sons under the age of six, (himself the eldest), had given Will a burning desire to succeed.

Joseph had some time on his hands now that the harvest was in, and so he went with Will to have a good look at the four-arched bridge over the widest part of the Owenreagh River at Shaneragh. Just below Dromore itself, they stopped at another bridge with a history.

In the old days, the cottage weavers from Drumquin forded a mountain stream at that spot to bring their famed linen yarn, tweeds and flax to the Dromore Fair. The Alexander family, who had settled the place a long time before, had recently encouraged their tenants to build a bridge at the ford. The tenants worked long and hard, believing the promise they had been given that no toll would ever be exacted for that bridge. On the first Fair Day of the next New Year, imagine the surprise of the villagers who found themselves face to face with a tollkeeper!

By ten o'clock that morning, a colourful parade of tenants and weavers had formed with marching bands and were headed down the road toward the now inaccessible Owenreagh Bridge.

In the meantime, landlord Alexander had called in a troop of horse soldiers and the local yeomanry. At noon, armed only with blackthorn sticks, and cheering wildly, the people drove the police and cavalry steadily back through the streets of the village.

Unfortunately, property was damaged and a policeman killed by a stray stone. Three men, Barrett, Gallagher and Hannigan, were transported to Van Dieman's Land in Australia and many others were forced to flee to safety. But the day the cavalry had to back off lived on in local legend.

The next morning Will went dutifully back to the more boring part of his task, counting houses; *twenty-nine of one-storey, sixty-eight of two-storeys, and five of three-storeys, mostly built of stone,* he noted down. Joseph broke in, "And there was the house in which a man named Kelly was murdered by Lieutenant Hamilton on a Fair Day just fourteen years ago when he shot into a crowd of innocent people." This certainly didn't fit under the headings Will was supposed to fill out, so he continued, *twenty-seven slated roofs and the remainder thatched.*

"Those roofs nearly all went up in flames when the notorious Lord Blayney and his dragoons came through here in search of rebels some years back," Joseph informed him. "The whole town might have gone up in flames if it hadn't been for our curate, Benjamin Marshall. He's the mildest mannered man you'd ever want to meet, but he stopped Blayney in his tracks with the help of a Captain and a Lieutenant who were horrified at his Lordship's actions."

"That same curate rushed into a burning house on that corner right over there to rescue a baby from its cradle where its terrified parents had left it. And now the daughter of that curate is married to one of the richest young men in Australia, one of the Osbornes."

As they continued down Main Street, Joseph told him who lived in each house: the Sproules, O'Briens, McCoys, Scotts, McCuskers, Fenlons, McMahons, Humphreys, McLoughlins, McAleers, and the Anthony family. Then there were the McGraths, James Gilmore the carpenter, James Slevin, one of the schoolmasters family of Slevins, Catherine and Denis Teague, Thomas Corry, Margaret Cunningham, Thomas Gallagher, and Breege McIlholm.

When they turned onto Church Street, John Scott, the tailor, teased Joseph Fleming about having a new suit made. "I'd never afford that, John," was the reply.

"Don't blame it on me if that waistcoat falls off you all by itself one of these days," John retorted. Indeed the britches Joseph habitually wore had turned almost grey from the lime dust embedded in the corduroy.

By the end of the day, Will had met nearly everybody in Dromore. They spent a little while in Cassidy's. Though Joseph did not drink alcohol, he sat comfortably swapping stories with the other men while Will listened. If the story was especially poignant, about two brothers who had killed each other over a woman, it was met with a Greek chorus of "oh, the pity of it," or "sad, indeed that was," encouraging the storyteller to continue with another one.

Will regretfully returned to the mundane task at hand. Under the heading 'Communication', he noted with some feeling: *It is notorious in the parish that half the number of roads actually contained in it would be more serviceable if kept in good repair than all the wretched lines which now intersect it in all directions.*

Indeed, he noted: *There has been little improvement in the parish of any kind for many years, because of the absence of proprietors and of the rector of the parish who had not lived in it for forty years back until three years ago when the present incumbent arrived.*

And twenty-one-year-old Will couldn't resist adding a cheeky comment of his own to amuse his superiors: *It is a singular fact that almost all the parishioners belonging to the Church of England are at heart mere Methodists, and though they appear at church in the morning, they never fail to season the information they derive there with a little Methodist rant in the evenings.* Never mind that his friend, Joseph, was a Methodist.

The Old Church on the Brae

Early the next morning, the two men climbed up to the Old Church on the Brae. Will admired the mullioned transept window. Joseph had patched some of the cracks around it, but more cracks were appearing, and the roof was obviously beyond repair. There was talk of a new church, but the rector was occupied with the fine new glebe house he was building for his large family. And on July 12ᵗʰ of that year he had tactlessly placed a large Orange flag on the church roof, and another one over the entrance to the graveyard where Catholics and Protestants lay side by side.

Joseph showed the younger man the grave of his own grandfather. *Thomas Fleming, born 1713, died aged 94 in 1807, son of John Fleming of Mulnagoe*, so the inscription read.

Will sensed the attachment this man had to this place and the people who had gone before him. He thought with regret of his own father, now living in grand style in Italy. He and his brothers had been obliged to go with their mother to live with their grandmother in the tiny Welsh hill village of St. Asaph, gateway to the picturesque vale of Clwyd, with the smallest ancient cathedral in the whole of Britain. All these years his mother had supported them with her poetry. How he wished he had had a father like Joseph.

His thoughts were interrupted by an apologetic cough. A man of middling height had entered the graveyard with another, who carried a large shovel over his shoulder. "Our curate, Mr. Marshall, who saved Dromore, and our friend to the end, Mr. Walsh." The gravedigger touched his cap then moved to his task.

Will murmured appropriate phrases but the sight of a new pit being dug opened up a raw wound. Only last May, he had watched his beloved mother being lowered into her own grave. *Felicia Browne Hemans, age 41*, the inscription read. She had died of tuberculosis in her tiny house on the edge of St. Stephen's Green. He had found her there. The only relative at the graveyard had been his uncle, now Chief Constable of Dublin's Metropolitan Constabulary. Felicia had come to Dublin to be near him.

Every schoolboy in the Empire probably knew her most famous poem by heart — at least the first two lines of it:

> *The boy stood on the burning deck,*
> *Whence all but he had fled.*[3]

He wanted those lines carved on her tombstone, but had been dissuaded by his uncle. Would anyone remember them ten, twenty years from now?

His mother had been a friend of the poet Wordsworth, had stayed with him and his sister, Dorothy, at Dove Cottage in England's Lake District. The great poet had praised her poetry, and her gentle spirit. She had won the hearts of a generation of Victorians who perhaps saw in her writing a reflection of their best selves. She had raised five sons, all the while a semi-invalid. Would even her name be remembered one hundred years hence?

Will looked around at the other graves, some unmarked, some with headstones leaning a little crazily to one side. Near

---

[3] *From the poem "Casabianca"*

the entrance a few were enclosed by a fine wrought iron railing, engraved with the name Noble. "Some of George's wealthier relatives, I believe, those who own their own land, unlike the rest of us," Joseph explained, with no trace of regret. Will thought of Jane, the young Jane Noble, who reminded him a little of his mother, with her dark hair, and of his new friends, George and Joseph. How strange, he thought, that the lives of these people I have just met should become so interwoven with mine, as though each of our stories is part of some greater whole, unfolding all the while. Curious that in this isolated village he should no longer feel so alone. A few days ago it was just a dot on a map.

It was peaceful, here on the Brae. Across the road, a few cows grazed placidly against the slope of the hill. One raised its head, stared at him, then bawled companionably. He almost laughed out loud, remembering his mother's favourite poem. He repeated the words slowly,

> *The curfew tolls the knell of parting day,*
> *The lowing herd winds slowly o'er the lea,*
> *The plowman homewards plods his weary way,*
>
> *...*

"Do you know it, Joseph?" he asked hopefully.

The older man nodded, "We learned it in school.

> *Now fades the glimmering landscape on the sight,*
> *And all the air a solemn stillness holds,*
> *Save where the beetle wheels his drowsy flight,"*
>
> ...

A cough tinged with merriment broke in on them. "I don't see a beetle anywhere, do you?" said the voice of the curate at his side. "Ah, but our Thomas Gray got it right, ***Elegy Written in a Country Churchyard*** and here we are.

> *Perhaps in this neglected spot is laid*
> *Some heart once pregnant with celestial fire;*
> *Some mute inglorious Milton here may rest,*
> *Some Cromwell, guiltless of his country's blood."*

"And ours, too," he muttered. "Would that it were true." And with that curate and gravedigger accompanied Will and Joseph back down the hill to the village.

On their arrival they heard a great commotion. People were running out of the shops toward one of the houses on Main Street. Two of the village's constables were striding purposefully in the same direction, soon to disappear though a front door now thrown wide open. Joseph followed. He knew the house well; his son, William, had often been a guest there. Its owner was Dr. W. who had been a surgeon on a man-of-war naval vessel for many years. William had enjoyed the man's stories. They were well told, enlivened by the fine classical education Dr. W. had gained in his early days at Trinity College. Recently, without explanation, William Fleming had ended the visits.

Before Joseph could find out what had happened, Dr. W. was led away in a straitjacket, half-supported by one of the burly constables. Joseph went into the house and found James Dill already there. This young Presbyterian minister had just arrived that August from Donegal, and already knew most of the people in the village.

Little by little Joseph learned the whole sorry story. The visits of the doctor to the local pub had become more frequent. "Yesterday morning the doctor's sister-in-law, a young girl, came across the street to my lodgings to request me to go over to see the doctor, who she said was very ill," Dill told him. "I found him in bed and apparently little the matter with him, except a tremor in his hand and a slight twitch of the lip. On my remarking, "You are not very ill," he replied, "You don't know what is the matter with me — it is the first stage of *delirium tremens*. I have had it three times before, and now while my reason remains, I want to prepare for the worst."

"I was absolutely astounded," young Dill told Joseph. "I read and prayed with him, pointed him to the Lamb of God who 'came into the world to save sinners, even the worst, whose blood cleanseth from all sin,' and besought him to flee to this only refuge of the sinner. I saw him again several times during the day; every time there was a change for the worse.

"Early this morning I was sent for in great haste. I ran across and there I beheld a sight I shall never forget — Dr. W. stood in his nightdress at his own bedroom door with a drawn dagger in his hand; his wife and sister-in-law had fled and he was pursuing them. I prevailed upon him to give me the dagger and to go into his bed, but every minute he started up, and with the most frightful gestures exclaimed, 'There they are, don't you see them!' The surgeon was able to shave his head. He became so violent soon after that the constables had to put him in a straitjacket, as you have seen, and I fear we will not cast our eyes upon him again except in death."

Joseph was more than usually silent as they rode homeward. Will was interested to learn more about the young preacher who had faced down an armed man. Later Dill would give a rousing speech on temperance to a cheering crowd of three thousand people in the new Catholic chapel, standing side by side with Fr. Theobald Matthew, the apostle of temperance from Cork. Before he went to bed Will added a self-righteous note to his report: *It may be noticed under the head, 'Habits of the People,' that there is a quantity of whisky drunk in this small place quite disproportionate to the number of the inhabitants, as the above table containing nineteen spirit shops out of forty-four tradesmen's houses will testify.*

The next evening, knowing Will would soon be leaving, the Nobles invited some of the neighbours. Will still had many questions and now threw one of them out. "Why is there so little new building in the village itself? Why are some of the houses in such disrepair?" The answer came with unexpected heat from William Fleming who had sat silent on two previous evenings. "I was just eight years old when two bad harvests in a row hit our part of the country, 1816 and 1817 that was. Some of my school friends were dying of the fever that followed on after. They closed the schools.

People sold their clothing for food — there were children running around naked. There was no dispensary then, no medicine except a few herbs, no doctor."

"People were just beginning to recover from that, those that did recover, when a second famine hit five years later. There's a cumulative effect to these things that takes the heart out of people. Do you wonder people don't worry about a bit of dirt or a broken-down wall?"

Will was intrigued by this man now suddenly so passionate. William was a fraction taller than his father, Joseph, equally broad-shouldered with black hair and deep set eyes. He had the bearing of a soldier but had never carried arms; his skin and roughened hands told of a life outdoors.

Now he continued. "On the other hand, we're luckier than many a village in Ireland. We've two good men who've landed in our midst. I take it you've been hearing of James Dill, our new young Presbyterian minister who came in here like a whirlwind from Donegal in August and was ordained this month. He's set us all back on our heels, including our new rector, who isn't used to a young upstart — just your age, Will, begging your pardon — stirring things up, and a non-conformist at that. And then there's our new Parish Priest, Father Peter Gordon, a cousin of old Benjamin Marshall whom I gather you met upon the Brae. Interesting man is Father Peter, son of a Protestant blacksmith, with his father's height and strength. He's gone about rebuilding the church with all that energy, and the willing help of his parishioners. He's even dragooned my father into helping them insert two lovely new windows, as I'm sure you've seen." Will nodded. He had noted down the rebuilding for his report in his usual laconic style.

On the last evening of his stay in Dromore, Will found himself wishing he had a painter's gift. Jane sat by the fire mending her lovely red cloak. It fell in folds of rich colour across the dark blue of her long wool skirt. The cloak had been made by her grandmother and given to her on her wedding day. She was just twenty-four years old, with silky black hair coiled loosely at the back of her head, clear skin tanned by hours in the fields and dark eyes that sparkled as she talked. Her nine-month-old baby, Eliza, lay fast asleep in a cradle at her feet. George stood leaning against the hearth, pipe in hand in a rare moment of relaxation. The blazing turf fire cast a ruby glow over the whole family, as though Will was looking at an old painting. He would remember them like this.

Back in Dublin, in his cubbyhole at Phoenix Park, Will reread his report. Pretty pedestrian stuff, he thought. For a moment he hesitated, then inserted one final paragraph. *One instance of peculiarity of costume prevails in this as well as in the surrounding parishes of this part of Tyrone, that is, the great prevalence of red cloaks and shawls among the women. At a fair or any other concourse of people this remark cannot fail of occurring to the stranger. Its effect is very pleasing in the crowd. It gives a great air of liveliness and brilliance to the fairs.*

With a flourish he signed his name, *Memoir by W. Hemans, 30ᵗʰ November, 1835.*

Perhaps someone else would see Dromore through different eyes ...

CHAPTER II

Polly Steps Out, 1839

Bridge Road, Dromore, January 6, 8:00 a.m.

"Where is that child going?" George Noble asked suddenly as he caught sight of a jaunty little person vanishing at rapid speed out the front door, wearing his favourite cap at an angle on her tousled brown hair.

"Polly, come back, you haven't finished your porridge," called her mother, Jane, without looking up. She was busy stirring a special cake for Little Christmas, 'Women's Christmas', they called it. All over Ireland women were preparing a special feast for their families.

"How on earth anyone can keep track of such a lively two-year-old is beyond me. I don't know where she gets all her energy. Probably from your side of the family," she said pointedly in the general direction of her husband.

George was only half-listening as he sat at a corner of the kitchen table calculating how many pigs he would have to sell this year to pay the heavy lease on his land that came relentlessly due every year. *The year of our Lord 1839, January 6th*, he wrote carefully at the top of the letter he was writing to the landlord. Already another year gone, he thought. And even though we are better off than some, with no debts and enough land for cows and horses, and bacon enough for ourselves and then some, we never seem to get ahead. If I make improvements, the rent can go up any time that miserable steward gets it in his head to raise his own standing with our big landowner. He came to with a start. "What is that you said about Polly? I'll go and look if that will set your mind at rest."

George looked fondly across at his wife who was showing Eliza, their eldest, now all of four years old, where to place currants in the fragrant cake. Jane had grown up on a farm near Enniskillen. Her father was a Fermanagh man, Thomas Caldwell. He married Mary Fair, who had relatives in Dromore (who used the old spelling of Phair). It was in their home that George had met Jane. They had been childhood sweethearts. As soon as she turned eighteen, he had proposed. Now he was worried about what would happen to them if his health failed. His chest still troubled him after the last drenching he got chasing a wayward cow. Shaking himself, he stood up, glad of an excuse to leave the bills and get out of doors.

"Run along with your father. The sun will do both of you good," Jane said indulgently. Eliza bolted for the door, glad of a reprieve from the morning's chores. How could anyone stay indoors on a day like this when the whole world had turned into a snowy white paradise? As Jane watched her go, she frowned slightly. This child had an elfin quality about her, with her light blonde hair, dancing pointed chin, grey eyes, and slight build. Already her head was full of stories she had heard, goodness knows where, and could tell off by heart. Her birth had been difficult, unlike Polly's, and Jane worried a little about her.

Eliza herself had not a care in the world as she skipped happily along beside her adored father, humming a little tune, tugging at his old brown wool shirt to get him to look at a rabbit burrowing through the new-fallen snow.

Polly was already out of earshot in fast pursuit of her little pet hen. She had stepped out into a white world, transformed overnight as if by magic. A heavy snow had fallen, a rare enough occurrence in Tyrone, and soon her little brown hen had turned into a ball of white fluff, scooting along on spindly yellow legs. Barn and byre had turned into a place fit for a princess, glistening and gleaming. The stalks in the far cornfield sparkled with a thousand diamonds of light.

George needn't have worried. Soon he saw Muff, the sheepdog, gently escorting her charge back where she belonged. Lucky the day he had found Muff, covered with mud, huddled in a ditch by the roadside. When her fur was cleaned she turned out to be a beautiful black and white border collie, abandoned no doubt by a careless owner on his way to winter elsewhere. Muff had adopted Polly as one of her own, to everyone's relief.

Dublin, 1839. 10:00 p.m.

That night of Little Christmas, their friend, Will Hemans, had been enjoying a comfortable dinner with his uncle George Browne. They had been celebrating Will's new job, building bridges under the tutelage of one of Ireland's most distinguished engineers. Neither had noticed the sudden drop of the barometer. At 10:30 when the storm broke, his uncle, now head of the Constabulary, was out the door like a shot, Will following him across the Carlisle Bridge,[4] where people were crawling across on their hands and knees. When he could at last stand upright, in a sudden eerie calm where hardly a candle flickered, his uncle was already out of sight.

Then suddenly, he saw two gigantic whirlwinds coming towards him from opposite ends of the street. He was in the middle of the worst storm in six hundred years. A tall chimney came crashing down almost at his feet, bringing part of the roof with it. He could have been killed. He learned next morning from the newspaper that a young man, "as he turned the corner of Sackville Street and Britain Street was blown off his feet, dashed against a lamp post and had his leg fractured in a most shocking manner." Will had escaped by a hair's breadth.

---

[4] *Later O'Connell*

All around him the city had the appearance of a war zone, streets blocked by fallen trees and debris, more than five hundred chimneys down and some of their roofs with them. As he turned a corner, he heard men shouting and nearly fell over a huge cannon being dragged towards what appeared to be a wall of flames.

It was the Bethesda Chapel, now a blazing inferno threatening to engulf the nearby House of Refuge for Reclaimed Females. The artillerymen had orders to bring down any adjoining walls to prevent a citywide conflagration, but they stood paralyzed — neighbouring houses were ablaze and one of them now came crashing down. Will saw his uncle amid the haze of smoke and rushed to help him and some of the soldiers bring the terrified women and children to safety. The fire burned well on into the next day before it was under control and only then did Will have a moment to wonder what had happened with his friends up north.

Bridge Road, Dromore, 10:00 p.m.

Earlier that afternoon, the weather had turned unexpectedly hot, the temperature rising steadily towards evening. The snow began to melt. It was so remarkably still that George could hear voices talking to each other a mile away across the valley. The horses in their stalls stirred restlessly. George was uneasy, but there had been none of the usual weather warnings. All day heavy copper clouds hovered, blocking out light and holding the heat in. At nine o'clock a light breeze promised relief.

Both children were fast asleep. Eliza in the outshot bed not far from the hearth. Jane and George sat quietly by the fire. All at once, at about 10:30, a noise like the screaming of a thousand banshees broke the eerie silence. As though the sky itself had cracked open, a violent wind rattled the house to its very foundation.

Every piece of Jane's wedding delph crashed down from the dresser shelves. The two front windows blew in, scattering the floor with shards of glass. There was an ominous cracking sound overheard, as though the central beams might give way. The chimney shook violently and then before Jane's horrified eyes, the hearth fire seemed to turn into an avenging figure of the Last Judgment, blowing a cloud of flame and cinders into the room. A tongue of flame ran up the side of the curtain of the outshot bed.

In a single motion, George tore down the curtain, snatched up Eliza and handed her to Jane. Roughly he pushed them towards the safety of the small bedroom where Polly lay sleeping, slammed the heavy oak door shut and snatched up a bucket of well water.

When Jane dared to come out, the hearth room had grown cold. The fire was out, the floor a sodden mass of ashes, shards of china and glass and burnt cloth. "At least we're alive, the children are safe!" Jane exclaimed, still shaking and shivering from shock.

George said nothing. He made sure the windows were well stuffed and barricaded in case the wind rose again. He looked in on the sleeping children, kissed Jane goodnight, and before she could stop him vanished out the door into the drenching rain to see to the horses. He had heard them screaming in the storm. To his amazement, he found the whole side of the barn down, partly demolished by the wind and the rest kicked out by an infuriated mare who was not about to let her offspring perish in the storm. Off she galloped, colt in tow, and as the storm clouds closed in once more, George heard the echo of a far-off wild whinny. She's in her true element, so she is, he thought.

Dromore, January 7

The next day, the entire population of Dromore was out in Main and Church Streets, marvelling that they were still here. The End of the World had not come, as many had feared. Some had run terrified and half-naked into the streets, only to be met with a hail of debris. Hayricks from every haggard had been lifted on the wind and blown through the streets and far into the countryside. A turf stack had been lifted a foot into the air and then dashed to pieces. No one knew what they owned anymore. All the streams and small loughs were clogged. The old church on the Brae, high above the town, had been severely damaged.

News was coming in from all over. Salt water had been tasted forty miles inland. The Strule at Omagh had flooded as usual, only more so. Cassidy's, the spirit dealer, stayed open, though all the shops and schools were shut, so that the stories could be told in a proper setting. Fish had been seen swimming down Omagh's High Street. One man swore he had seen an old lady hanging onto the tail of her cow as it swam past him. Two coffins had been dragged upright at Ballylesson. No one knew whether to laugh or cry.

Up on Bridge Road, Jane sat quietly by the bedside of her husband, now tossing with fever in a fitful sleep. He had come back in the early morning, all but one of the horses safe, but himself chilled to the bone. A coughing fit had seized him and nothing she could do would stop it. Late that evening the village surgeon, Dr. Marshall, came by, but he only shook his head. There was little they could do now except wait.

Jane's mother came to stay with her. At 3:00 a.m. four days later, Jane wakened from an exhausted sleep, her mother's gentle hand on her shoulder. "He's gone," was all she said.

Neighbours came by, bringing food and comfort and news of the storm that continued to come in from all directions. Jane found something consoling in hearing these stories, as though it made her own loss more bearable. Others were worse off, she could tell herself. In Grenshaw, a mother and her three daughters were killed by a house falling in. In Loughrea, eighty-seven houses had burned to ashes. From Galway and all along the coast came news of ships sunk, bodies washed ashore. A million beautiful trees had been uprooted.

In all the general devastation, the individual stories were most poignant: the watchman in Belfast who was killed when one of the tallest mill towers came crashing down, leaving one small son and his widow penniless; and the weavers of Tallaght who had silently looked at the ruins of their homes on Killenarden Hill, pounded to smithereens by their own looms broken loose, and then had walked away without a word, no one knew where.

And from nearby Belcoo, a letter in the *Enniskillen Chronicle and Erne Packet* that Jane's mother read to her:

> *It is hard to conceive and impossible to describe the melancholy effects of this awful storm in this neighbourhood.*

Few houses, if any, have escaped, several families were obliged to take shelter at the back of ditches, whilst their tottering cabins threatened destruction, and having fallen caught fire from the cinders and were burned with their contents. One poor man has lost his life — four cows were killed on the property of Mr. Hugh Bracklin — whole stacks of corn, in several instances were carried off and destroyed, whilst hay, straw and turf are to be seen everywhere scattered through the fields. But the most lamentable object to be seen in the general ruin is the Holywell Chapel. This beautiful edifice, the ornament of a wild and barren mountain, the object of the peculiar care of a numerous and poor people, which for years they had been struggling to raise, and which they had now almost finished in a manner, even beyond their means, suited to the worship of the most High, this their great earthly comfort is the most melancholy instance of the irresistible fury of the late storm. The wind having forced open the western door made its way through the roof on the north side and carried off timber, slates, ridge and barge courses, which are to be found at a mile's distance broken in pieces or ground into dust. The roof on that side is totally gone — the principals only remain, whatever had been left on the south side is falling by degrees. It is really distressing to see the poor people today going about this sad ruin sighing and wailing.

Jane and her mother had often gone to the Holywell near the chapel where people had come for centuries to find healing. It was a place she had loved as a child. The ice-cold water coming in a never-ending stream from deep in the earth, springing up into eternal life, she always thought as she sat there watching, as she had sat that long night beside the bed of her beloved husband.

Neighbours came quietly to Jane's aid. Potatoes were set and dug, corn planted and harvested. Jane was well loved and respected for her open-heartedness and simplicity. She determined to run the farm as best she could.

Eliza was the only one who could remember their father clearly, a man who now seemed to Polly like someone in a dream. Together with their mother they brought flowers that summer to his grave in the Noble compound in the old churchyard. There never seemed time to arrange for a marker. All of Jane's energy went into the never-ending daily tasks.

Occasionally she and the children stopped to watch Joseph Fleming and the other stonemasons as they attempted to repair the damage done to the old church by the Big Wind. It was a thankless task. Most of the roof and part of one wall had been badly damaged. All of the lovely old glass windows had been smashed to smithereens. By the end of the summer, however, enough repairs had been done to allow services to resume.

Jane and her mother at Holywell, Belcoo.

CHAPTER III

William Fleming Proposes, 1840

Early one September day, Jane was out in the yard feeding the hens when she heard the clatter of hooves. It was William Fleming from across the road. She couldn't help noticing what an attractive figure of a man he was, astride a frisky young draught horse, which he controlled with a light touch. She also knew from local gossip that he spent quite a lot of time playing cards with some of the wealthier local lads. It was from one of them he had won this fast horse, named Ahasuerus, which was now a favourite in the small local races on the flat ground outside Dromore. Having two horses was an unheard of luxury among the neighbouring farms. Every local mother with an unmarried daughter had her eye on widower William, but so far he had shown no sign of settling down again. Yet each time there was a crisis on Jane's farm, he had turned up. It was clear the horses welcomed the sound of his voice. Now all he said was, "a few of the neighbours are coming tonight to celebrate my father's

William (1807-1876) and Jane Cauldwell (1811-1871) Fleming.

seventieth birthday. I know Polly has become a special favourite of his. We'd be honoured if the three of you would celebrate with us." Jane accepted with alacrity. It would be a welcome change from the long days of hard work running both farm and household, and keeping track of two lively children who just now were racing noisily across the field to avoid the crabby old billy-goat.

A year later, to no one's surprise except their own, William and Jane were engaged. Joseph made no secret of his delight. "You'll be a good steadying influence on William," he whispered to Jane. "I know he's been a little wild since he lost his first wife and newborn child, but there is a largeness of spirit in the man that has not shown itself yet." The wedding was set for October 15, 1841.

While all the preparations were going on, Eliza and Polly went to stay with their grandparents in Fermanagh. Jane's mother, Mary

Fair Caldwell, was an indulgent grandparent, much less strict about things like bedtime than their mother. To their delight, their Uncle Sandy Fair had just arrived for one of his rare visits from London where he was a Scottish guard at Queen Victoria's court. He brought his sister a reproduction of the new portrait of the young queen. Polly studied it carefully. Victoria had come to the throne in 1837, the year Polly was born. She thought the young queen looked rather sad and overwhelmed by the task ahead of her, and decided then and there that being a queen was not much fun.

Polly's sister and closest friend thought otherwise. Eliza looked a little like a princess herself, with her light golden hair that came from her mother's side of the family. She adored romantic stories, but she soon discovered that Polly was bored by passive princesses cooped up in towers waiting to be rescued by a male hero, so she began storing away tales to intrigue this small sister with brown hair that always refused to curl. Their grandfather, John Caldwell, and his neighbour, Mr. McElholm, knew many of the old Scottish and Irish Celtic stories. Eliza could repeat almost word for word everything she heard from him and the older neighbours. And so Polly heard about the kingdom of Dalriada that once stretched from the top of Ireland right over into Scottish Argyle.

Most memorable in Polly's view was the sorrowful tale of Fionnuala, the daughter of Lir, turned into a swan for nine hundred years along with her three brothers by a jealous stepmother. Waving a Druid's wand, the four children were allowed to spend the first three hundred years close to home where their heartbroken father and grandfather could come to see them. They kept their own children's voices, and people from all over Ireland came to hear their beautiful music.

But then they were condemned to fly for three hundred years over the cold and stormy waters of the Irish Sea. When at last after another three hundred years the spell was broken, their wizened faces frightened each other.

And now, to keep Polly from being lonesome away from home, in the big bed in the loft of their grandparents' house, Eliza whispered another story to her from olden times of three Scottish princesses who fell in love with three Irish princes. Eliza rose to her full height, waved her arms with the drama of it all, her golden hair shimmering in the moonlight as she described the tragedy, the death of the three princes in battle, and the heartbreak of the three princesses as they turned their faces into the ground to die on the spot of grief. Polly wiped a tear from her eyes as the glorious story ended, then promptly fell asleep, curled up beside her sister in the old house with an owl hooting gently outside in the starlit night.

When the girls returned home there was great bustle and comings and goings as Jane prepared for the wedding. She would have preferred to have young James Dill perform the ceremony. She had become close to his wife, Sarah, who like herself had been widowed at a young age. The two of them had shared many a laugh and a shiver at James's insistence on moving his new family into the most notoriously haunted house in the area.

There was still, however, some lurking question about the validity of marriages conducted by Presbyterian clergy, much to young Dill's annoyance. And so Jane was married in her home by Rector Henry Lucas St. George, thirty years older than Dill, and seemingly already set in his ways.

For days before the wedding, Jane worried how on earth she was going to keep the two men well apart. The very public letter feud in the northern newspapers between them over a minor incident in the parish of Dromore had kept the neighbourhood amused for weeks. She needn't have worried.

Just as the rector pronounced William and Jane man and wife there was a clatter of hooves accompanied by shouts and shrieks of laughter. A band of the younger Presbyterian farmers galloped up, late for the wedding and not in the least apologetic. Some of their horses had accidentally skittered into the large open cesspool at the edge of the village. The dresses of the ladies, the britches of the men and flanks of the horses were splattered with the reeking stuff. No one would forget this wedding in a hurry.

Once Jane and the children had settled into their new home across the road at Bridgewater Farm, Sarah Dill came over for a visit and a good laugh.

"I can tell that living with a Fleming will never be dull," Jane confided. "The local gossips are at pains to tell me that Patrick Fleming was a well known outlaw in these parts, one of the rapparees. Ironic when it was the Flemings who helped the Normans conquer the English in 1066. They say Patrick and his fellow rapparees only stole what they needed to survive. Then there was Redmond Fleming, another outlaw who lived by his wits and only just escaped prison. People have long memories in these parts. They talk as if this all happened just yesterday."

"Now the gossips love to tell me there is a Fleming running an illegal still on the island in Aughlish Lough, making a potent and popular brand of poteen from potatoes, right under the nose of the constables. Joseph just shakes his head when I ask him about it."

Sarah sympathized with the delights and problems of a second marriage. Her young husband, James Dill, in addition to the letter-war with the rector, had recently stumbled on a cure for cancer. People were beginning to knock on their door at all hours of the night.

CHAPTER IV

The Bridgewater Years, 1841-1847

These first years at the farm were undoubtedly the happiest and most carefree of Polly's life. She could tell how contented her mother was in her new role. And then there was Joseph. From the first moment she had met him, Polly had adopted Joseph as her grandfather.

Just over six feet tall, with ruddy cheeks, keen grey-blue eyes and the weather-beaten skin of a man who had worked out of doors all his life, Joseph had an easy way with children, animals, and strangers at the door. In earlier years, if he wasn't ploughing, sowing and harvesting his own fields, he was over at a neighbour's, comfortable both giving help and asking for it when need arose. He paid little attention to clothes, quietly resisting all his wife's well-meaning efforts to get him spruced up. "That old shirt is going to fall off your back by itself if you don't watch out," Molly would scold.

"Leave me be, woman," he would say good-naturedly, giving in only on Sundays, fair days, and occasionally for company.

Bridgewater Farm was often full of visitors, some dropping by after milking time. Even after his wife's death, Joseph continued their tradition of hospitality. Since he had hurt his leg and still limped slightly, he went about less at night. One by one people turned up to talk, sure of a listening ear.

Within weeks of their arrival, Polly and Eliza had explored every inch of the farm's sixteen-and-a-half acres. They spent hours racing twigs on the Laughing Brook, a tiny stream that ran right across the bottom of the lower field, jumping back and forth to see who could leap the furthest without getting wet.

When it rained, they could curl up in the big loft over the kitchen, near the warmth of the central hearth chimney. At the far end of the loft were two small gable windows, one of which opened on a hinge. From those windows, Polly and Eliza could follow all the comings and goings on the coach road. And on long winter evenings, the loft with its high bog-oak beams could be transformed into a stage for high drama.

The house itself had been built about 1790 of white-washed fieldstone, set firmly into the solid rock of the hillside, by John Fleming, Joseph's father, a master stone mason like himself. As was the custom, John had the help of many of their neighbours. Because of its location, it had weathered the Big Wind fairly well, although part of the thatched roof had been sent flying over the farthest field. Originally the house had been a single storey high, but when Joseph's wife, Molly, gave birth to their fourth lively son, he added the loft to accommodate children, cousins and assorted visitors.

What with harvest festivals, her mother's wedding on October 15, and Halloween, that autumn seemed to Polly like one long celebration. On the evening of October 31, Joseph set a half-barrel on the stone floor of the kitchen, filled it with water, and with William's help, strung apples over the tub. Some of the neighbours' children came over for 'Snap Apple' night, as a few of them called it. Polly was beginning to feel as though this had been her home forever.

And Christmas was coming soon. But first the house had to be scoured from top to bottom, dishes and pots scrubbed, clothes and bedding washed, the yard swept, and the house freshly whitewashed inside and out. At the side of the house, Joseph had constructed a narrow channel so that when Jane went to teem the potatoes, the boiling water from the heavy iron pot could run off down the slope of the yard. This channel also received a good sweeping so that no debris clogged it.

Then came the best part. Eliza and Polly went hunting for holly branches in the nearby woods, and when they returned home the house was redolent with the smell of freshly baked bread, plum cake and pies. On the night before Christmas, as they worked frantically to finish the last of their homemade presents, they could smell the festive goose cooking. There would be beef as well, and vegetables grown right there on the farm. The whole family had gone together to the Christmas market in Omagh, known as the Margadh Mor[5]. They returned home with sugar, spices and toys.

---

[5] *The Big Market held at this time throughout most of Ireland*

That first Christmas every inch of space was needed as relatives began to arrive from all directions. Jane's parents came of course, eager to inspect their new son-in-law at close quarters, bringing with them Jane's younger brother, John Caldwell, and his wife Margaret. They were just about to emigrate to the Province of Canada on the far side of the Atlantic and were full of glowing reports of opportunities there.

Jane privately could think of nothing worse than leaving friends and kinfolk and the familiar fields of home to embark on such a risky venture with her children, but she kept her thoughts to herself. Everything important to her was wrapped up in this Christmas celebration with the people she loved.

Once Christmas was over, Polly counted the days until she could get out in the fields again for spring planting. The land on this farm sloped gently downhill, giving a view far far away to the Sperrin Mountains.

Traditionally, for the neighbours up and down the coach road the feast day of St. Brighid, on the first of February, was the beginning of the farming year and there were many interesting rituals attached to that day. A few of their friends kept to the old way of coming together out in the field to turn the first sod and say one of the traditional prayers. Woe betide the man who started ploughing before all that was done properly. Joseph treasured a St. Brighid cross that had been given to him by a neighbour when he was a little boy. And when Polly went into Dromore with her mother at this season, she counted the number of St. Brighid crosses tucked into the thatched roofs of the houses. Sometimes there were as many as twenty or thirty.

Jane was always fascinated by the variety of ploughs that were used by the men on the nearby farms. She had offered George's old plough to William but he already had one of the newer Scotch ploughs and was out early to hitch up the Irish cob named Clara, a sturdy broad-beamed horse bred for heavy farm work. It was immensely satisfying to him to see the earth drawn into long straight furrows. In a wet season, a field could easily become clogged with clay, slowing the work down, but William always had a sharpened stick with him to clear out the spokes.

Next the sods had to be broken up and flattened down with a roller. Then came the harrowing. When that was done it was time for the sowing of the grain. Polly had been waiting for this moment for days. Nothing pleased her more than to find herself out in the field, commissioned by her new grandfather to shoo the crows and fowl away from the newly sown grain, walking a few paces behind him as he hand-sowed the oats from the depths of an old apron. Despite teasing from his family, he refused to use a proper sowing fiddle which would have speeded things up considerably.

The Bog

That year, after the March winds and lengthening days dried the surface of the bog, Joseph went ahead to prepare their allotted section for cutting. With a spade and a sharp nicking-tool, he pared off about a foot of the tough grasses, heather and moss, exposing the dark peat below. Next he spread the top layer carefully to give a dry footing for William and the other barrow-men who would wheel away the turves .

The next morning, Polly and Eliza helped their mother prepare a hearty ten o'clock tea for the men, who had been away by dawn. Slices of freshly baked bread with butter and homemade berry jam were packed into the wicker basket. Much to Polly's indignation, children her age weren't usually allowed to go on their own to the bog. It was too dangerous, with the deep water-filled bog holes. But now she would see for the first time the place where generations of Flemings had cut their winter fuel.

As they walked down over the sloping fields and across the stream on the rickety wooden bridge that held only one person at a time, they met other families they hadn't seen for awhile. What with stopping to catch up on the latest news and admire new babies who couldn't be left behind, they were almost late. The men, who had already been hard at work, were formed up into 'spades' of three. One of the three carried a murderous-looking long-handle spade called a slane, whose knife-like edge had been ground to razor sharpness, able to slice downwards through the mass of decayed roots. Joseph had chosen his slane carefully many years before, well aware, like the other men, that an ounce of weight or an inch of length could make the critical difference between a smooth cut and back-breaking labour. The local spade factory in nearby Fintona carried more than two hundred different sizes and shapes of spades, to suit the height and size of each man.

Jane first set the jars of fresh water and buttermilk for the men into a rough hole cut out of the side wall of the bank, where they would keep nicely cool. Next she brought Polly and Eliza to a safe distance from the bog-hole, made sure they saw where it was, and warned sternly, "If you go any closer, a man keeper will jump down your open mouth and choke to you death." Enough said. Only much later did Polly realize the small creatures wriggling beneath the surface of the dark water were perfectly harmless little newts.

The bank in this corner of the bog had been cut away quite deeply over the years. William was standing, legs braced, knees bent, on this lower level not far from the bog hole. High above them on the crest of the bank stood Joseph. As each turf was cut, he flung it down to his son, the catcher. The heavy black peat was sodden with a winter's rain, a single piece weighing anything up to ninety pounds.

Eliza whispered to Polly as they watched, "Look at Grandfather away up there standing against the sky with the clouds behind him.

Doesn't he just remind you of our giant Finn MacCool throwing mud like that across the Irish Sea at the Scottish giant? And next thing you know there's the Isle of Man in the middle of the sea, and the Giant's Causeway with its fantastic shapes. Wouldn't I just like to see that someday!"

For William there was nothing the least bit romantic about what he was doing. It was back-breaking work, strong as he was. And to make matters worse, his father flatly refused to buy a new hand-barrow to bring the turf out of the bog to the waiting cart. The old barrow was good enough for his father and grandfather, wasn't it? When William tried to push the thing, the barrow creaked along protesting, its heavy load sometimes lurching to one side, straining his shoulder muscles, its wooden sides patched together with odd bits of wire and wood that could drive a splinter into your hand if you weren't careful. His new bride didn't help by laughing at the gloomy expression on his face, as he muttered, "Waste not, want not indeed!"

William eventually decided to take matters into his own hands. Just before Eliza's birthday in May, he disappeared on a mysterious errand. On the day itself, Eliza and her young friends and cousins were playing outside in the cobbled yard when they heard the scuffling of small feet coming up the lane. The tiniest donkey Eliza had ever seen came plodding along towards them, with William close behind it. It headed straight for the open doorway of the house before he could stop it. This donkey had a mind of its own. It clambered awkwardly over the threshold and into the kitchen, where it had smelled food. Polly was inside, just about to carry out the plum cake Jane had prepared.

Startled by this apparition, this unfamiliar long-faced creature larger than herself, she started to back away and would have dropped the cake had not her mother snatched it from her. In no time at all donkey and child were fast friends and sharing a piece of cake. Polly even rode occasionally upon its back, on those rare occasions when it wasn't hard at work earning its keep.

Confessing himself smartly outmanoeuvered by his son, Joseph built a fine new cart for the donkey over the next winter. He had the help of his friend, Alf Crozier, the new blacksmith, an expert at turning out the best wheels around, an art in itself.

Alf often complained about the shortage of coal, since it best absorbed and held the oxygen from the great bellows. There was some coal on the market from Coalisland, but it was often hard to come by. The rest had to be brought by the new steamers from England, a chancy business at best. For a good part of the year he made do with a charcoal fire from peat charred in the pits; a peat fire itself could not long hold the air from the bellows without scattering.

Later in the spring, Jane took the children back to the bog. She and Eliza had work to do. Each of the heavy turves had to be spread out singly on the heather so one side could dry, then turned a bit later so the other side had a chance. Next came the most interesting part: four turves were up-ended and leaned together with a fifth laid carefully across the top. It was called footing the turf, to allow the drying wind to blow through. The resulting rickle looked very much like an ancient dolmen, an impressive sight when the surface of the bog was covered with these pre-historic shapes.

Within a couple of years, Polly would become quite expert at this task, but this year her one and only attempt at a rickle was an infuriating failure. Later when the rickles were dry, they were piled up in clamps. They could either be left in the bog until needed or brought home to the turf shed.

All these trips to the bog were time-consuming, back-breaking work for the adults, but they were a change of pace, a companionable time with neighbours. Polly and the younger children could run bare-footed among the heather, avoiding the sections that had been burned and hurt their feet. Eliza and the older children who did the harder tasks complained of rag nails so bad their fingers bled. There were sore backs and aching muscles. But everyone agreed that tea never tasted so good. Polly would remember for the rest of her life those sun-filled days, with the delicate white blossoms of the bog cotton nodding in the fresh wind all around her. Later when the rickles had dried, came the satisfaction of trudging home behind the heavily laden cart through meadows of long grass filled with buttercups, daisies and her favourite, the small lilac-coloured cuckoo flowers. And some years there was a trip or two in midsummer back to the bog when the digging and drying had been delayed.

Each day from the beginning of April, Polly peered anxiously at the ash tree at the bottom of the garden. Grandfather had told her, "When you can still see daylight through the ash trees it will be time to plant the potatoes." This was all very well, but how you could be sure? The truth was, you couldn't. This whole business of when to plant crops was a mysterious combination of weather-watching, intuition and years of experience.

All winter long Joseph and William held lengthy discussions about the best method of preparing the ridges. If Joseph had had his way, they would have spade-dug the whole acre of potatoes. He maintained to his dying day that this produced the best yield. "But I have to admit," Polly heard him say one night, "that horse of yours saves us both a lot of work." And well he knew that William was happiest when he was working closely with a horse.

At long last the day came for planting. Joseph picked up the heavy wooden bucket filled with seed potatoes while Polly trotted along beside him chattering happily. Over the winter the mound of cattle and pig manure had grown steadily beside the barn. It had been well mixed with lime and bog mud and spread over the field.

When Polly arrived at the first of the ridges, she found that she had to scramble into the ditch then climb up over the heavy sods that had been flipped over the side of the beds until she could place the first potato into the oozing mixture of fertilizer and mud, all the while holding the rest of the potatoes as best she could in her folded-up bag apron. It was no mean feat, given her age and size, and it soon became difficult to distinguish where her apron began and the ridge ended.

It was tiring work, all this scrambling in wet, cold mud. Soon her hands were numb and she was glad enough when Joseph sent her back to the house to fetch some tea for them both. When she returned, she found that he had quietly turned the seed potatoes so that the eyes were on top and a diamond pattern appeared all the way along the row. Three weeks later, he and William earthed up the beds, covering the spuds, so the ridges would drain well.

Polly was a little nervous as she entered the house, wondering what her mother would say when she saw her daughter spattered from head to toe with mud and dung. Jane just laughed and pulled out the heavy wooden tub from its hiding place, filled it with warm water from the big iron pot hanging over the fire and beckoned her daughter. Never had a bath felt so good! Polly decided then and there to postpone full employment as a potato setter until another year. "People call these lazy beds, but I don't see what's so lazy about them: that's hard work," remarked Polly, as her mother scrubbed the back of her neck until it was sore.

Wash-day

Polly couldn't for the life of her figure out why her mother found wash-day so satisfying. It came round relentlessly every Monday. All day long water was on the boil and the huge wooden buckets were filled with soapy water, sheets, pillowcases and the week's dirty clothes. Then came the scrubbing on the old wooden washboard, scrubbing till your fingers were raw and red, with the big bars of soap that came from James Browne's Soap Factory in Donaghmore. Last but not least, a final swish through cold water that just about froze your fingers off in winter.

The sheets and pillowcases were spread out on the egg-tree branches and left there at least one night to whiten, all the better if it turned out to be a frosty night. If it were a full moon that night, Eliza and Polly could look out and see their poke bag pillowcases looking like so many white ghosts. When they came down in the morning all the chairs and stools would be covered with clothes drying by the fire.

Once you lifted the clothes off, you had better not leave that empty chair with its back to the fire or it would bring you bad luck. Polly wasn't quite sure if she really believed this, but it was like not walking under a ladder, you got into enough trouble without bringing more of it on yourself.

On Tuesdays, Jane would get up early and the whole house would smell of freshly baking purdy bread, mingled with the smell of newly washed sheets. Then there was the game of hide-and-seek to find where the hens had laid their eggs and persuade them to let you have the smooth still-warm egg hidden under their feathers.

Jane made extra money by selling most of the eggs. Sometimes she took them to the market in Dromore, but often she preferred to take them to one of the four little country stores in the neighbourhood. Jane was sure of coming home with all the latest news almost before it happened.

Polly could never see why a little mud could hurt. In summer there was nothing better than feeling the satisfying squish of mud between your bare toes, and if a little of it found its way on your clothes what of it. Besides, her mother and her new papa were always laughing about what happened at their wedding.

The Sycamore

On days that did not go so well, like wash day, Polly had a special friend she could count on, the old sycamore that stood between the farmhouse and the coach road.

That old sycamore. It had been battered by many a storm, becoming a little more gnarled and bent each time, but still it stood, offering shade in summer and a bright flash of gold in autumn. That first winter on the farm, when she was just four, she had watched the tree gradually turning black in the late afternoon sun, a proud silhouette, a friend in the dusk, the leaves of the highest branches tipped with light.

If you stared at the tree long enough, she thought, you might gradually become part of it, reaching up towards heaven through its leaves. That never quite happened, much to her regret. But one hot August evening the following year, she was sent to bed for some minor infraction. She was leaning out of one of the two gable windows of the loft as far as she dared. Joseph had attached a hinge to it so that his grandchildren might benefit from fresh air, their one free commodity.

The summer scents were intoxicating; clover, honeysuckle and new-mown hay, with a dash of pungent manure. The grasshoppers and cicadas were in full throat. A fox barked in the distance; horses' hooves clopped on the dry roadbed. The sycamore, her friend, loomed as a dark silhouette against the western sky. Away down the slope of the nearest field a single blackbird had begun his evening song. It floated clear and high above the hum of insects, so powerful that in the end Polly heard nothing else, leaning into the song as though she had become part of it, a melody half-heard, half-remembered, going on all around her, whose meaning she couldn't quite grasp.

And then the song ended, and the evening star came out, a moment she would remember for the rest of her life.

For Polly, the farm and its fields were the core of an inner compass. North were the Sperrin Mountains in all their splendour and mystery, with the little stream in the middle distance. East was the bog turning purple and mauve in autumn, white with bog cotton in spring. South was the winding road, with the magical town of Enniskillen in the distance, a town she had seen only once.

And, perhaps best of all, west was the great sycamore tree, its branches backlit with golden fire when the sun set, if you forgot to remember the rainy days.

The sycamore on the old coach road.

CHAPTER V

Mrs. McAlistair Arrives, 1842

Early in the year, it became clear to Jane that she was expecting a baby. William was beside himself with joy and anxiety; after all, it was the birth of a child that had cost his first wife her life. Jane tried to reassure him, but her episodes of morning sickness had the opposite effect. Finally she decided to call on the help of a cousin of her mother's who had come to her aid after the difficult time she had with Eliza's birth. It was a decision she was to regret more than once.

Mrs. McAlistair, as everyone always called her, arrived with a flourish and a lot of baggage. It looked as though she meant to stay awhile. She was a large-boned woman with reddened hands, an ample bosom kept tightly under control, brown hair that unexpectedly refused to stay in its bun, and a way of looking down her nose at small persons that immediately made you feel guilty of something, or so Polly felt.

Mrs. M. clearly approved of Eliza, with her gentle ways and willingness to help with the most menial of household tasks. From the first moment she laid eyes on Polly, however, she had said to herself, "There's trouble; this child must not be spoiled." No matter how hard Polly tried, everything she did went wrong. She put too much pepper in the soup, so that the whole family took to sneezing; tore the sleeve of her best linen blouse an hour before church; and as spring turned into summer, was almost always late for supper.

One fateful evening, Polly had been sent to bed with no supper. Hungry and furious, she had lain awake until she was sure Mrs. McAlistair would be asleep by the fire as usual. Jane had smiled to herself as she saw the small shadow slipping out the door of the outshot pantry. Easygoing herself, she supposed a little discipline did no harm to her youngest. However, that night luck was not on Polly's side; there was a huge crash as Polly knocked over a pail of fresh milk that Mrs. McAlistair had brought in from the byre.

Within seconds, a large red hand had grasped Polly by the collar and dragged her to the nearest stool, where she was told to kneel down and ask God's forgiveness for her wicked disobedience. Blinking back the tears, Polly did as she was told, but there and then she decided she didn't much like this God of Mrs. McAlistair's, if He was spying on you all the time.

Heedless of further punishment, she ran out the front door. She was still sobbing when she arrived at the bottom of the last field where the little brook burbled along as though nothing in the world could possibly be wrong. In the sheltered corner of a rock near the brook, there was a tiny white narcissus growing. Polly had the strongest impression it had an important message to say to her, but she couldn't quite grasp what it was.

Angrily, she waded ankle-deep into the running water of the little stream. The coldness of the water stung her skin. As she stood there, her tears drying on her cheeks, a tiny tadpole swam past, for all the world as though it were going somewhere important. And then another. One of them swam confidingly into her cupped hand, its small velvet body wriggling with delight. She let it go, feeling her whole body relax as she did so.

She heard a rustle of footsteps in the grass. It was her mother, come to find her. "It's safe to come home now, Polly," she called gaily. "Mrs. McAlistair has fallen fast asleep. William has brought in a fresh pail of milk, and cleaned up the spill, and we're going to tell Mrs. M. that she dreamed the whole thing." Jane was laughing like a young girl, cheeks blooming, eyes dancing. Polly had seldom seen her mother look prettier.

In mid-August, Jane sent William galloping through the night for their favourite midwife, Mrs. Corey, who lived at Shaneragh. A few hours later, a tiny boy made his way into the world with a lusty yell. William was beside himself with relief and joy. After a whispered conference with Jane, he announced the baby's name would be Joseph. He had not even dared to think of a name until that moment.

To everyone's surprise, Mrs. McAlistair entered so wholeheartedly into the family's rejoicing that she forgot to scold her small target, Polly. Holding her tongue, albeit with some difficulty, she fussed

POLLY OF BRIDGEWATER FARM

over Jane and the baby, presided over wash-day and generally did the work of three people in one day.

To Polly's surprise, she even heard Mrs. McAlistair laugh one day, right out loud. And for once, she took off her apron, her badge of honour, as she called it, and accompanied the family to Fair Day on September 29. William couldn't wait to show off his son, and insisted on carrying him the whole way as they walked to the village, joined at every laneway by other families.

And a gay occasion it was. Throngs of fair-goers were already crowding Church and Main Streets, mixing with dealers and clowns, cows and squealing pigs. Braying donkeys contended with small boys shouting. The weavers showed off their frieze, drugget and linen to the best advantage, next to the cooper with his churns, noggins and firkins; all contending for buyers with the basket-maker, shoemaker and ever-present tinker. William bought Jane a bright red plaid shawl from one of the Drumquin weavers, to go with her red cloak. She fastened it with the brooch he had given her on their wedding day. Both of them noticed that some of the houses had been repaired since their friend, Will Hemans, had done his survey. Farmers were expecting a good harvest. It was a joyous occasion.

That Sunday, they all went to church together, not just once but twice. In the morning they trooped off to the old church on the Brae, where the organist did his best with the pipes of the ancient organ, and the soprano sang just a touch off key. That Sunday Mr. Marshall, the faithful curate, had picked Psalm 104 for one of the readings. Polly listened to the sheer poetry of the cadences:

Who covereth thyself with light as with a garment;
Who stretchest out the heavens like a curtain;
Who layeth the beams of his chambers in the waters;
Who maketh the clouds his chariot;
Who walketh upon the wings of the wind.

Polly sincerely hoped Mrs. McAlistair was listening properly, though she doubted it. Such a God would be much too busy to have time to spy on a small person like herself.

During the sermon, which was long and rather dull, Polly amused herself by watching the rain dripping from the leaky old roof down the back of the neck of the smallest Osborne boy who sat with his family in the front pew. There were fewer and fewer Osbornes now in that pew, with so many leaving for foreign parts to make their fortune.

In the afternoon, they all trooped off to the little Togherdoo Methodist Chapel for the once-a-month service with a visiting circuit preacher. Polly loved to hear the old hymns. William had a fine baritone voice and Mrs. McAlistair produced a surprisingly mellow contralto. Mrs. Gibson, whose family had given the land for the church, sang the soprano; Mr. Crozier, the blacksmith, came thundering in with the baritone. Eliza had a clear sweet voice. Polly simply could not keep a tune to save her life, but just listening to the lovely melodies sounding all around her was satisfaction enough.

As the service drew to a close, her favourite hymn soared out over the fields: *Praise, my soul, the King of Heaven.* No one could be unhappy while they were singing that. The words had been written by Henry Francis Lyte, whose family lived not far from Jane's family home. He had been a schoolboy at the Portora Royal School, set high on the hill at the west end of Enniskillen, overlooking the gently flowing River Erne. There was something in the very air of Fermanagh, among its vast expanse of lake and hill that had inspired many a writer. Two weeks before his death by tuberculosis in the fateful year of 1847, Henry Francis Lyte would write the words of *Abide with Me,* a hymn that has comforted people in many countries around the world.

CHAPTER V

Excursion to Andrew Fleming's Mill

That autumn when the oats were all in, Joseph invited Polly along for the ride to the corn mill. By rights they should be going to the nearest mill owned by their landlord. It was clearly understood by all parties concerned, however, that Joseph would take his oats to the mill in Shaneragh East run by his younger brother, Andrew. There were some things you didn't argue about with Joseph.

From quite a distance they could hear the noise of the great mill wheel as it turned. As they came closer the noise increased, a great grumbling, thundering, moaning, and creaking sort of a sound that entered right into the very marrow of your bones. Polly was completely enchanted. She had never heard or seen anything like it in her life. That month there had been a lot of rain, and the big wheel shuddered in its turning as the water poured in from the mill race.

Andrew Fleming was a great giant of a man, who could heave the sacks of meal over his shoulder as though they were rag dolls. He would live to be one hundred and ten. He and Joseph were close, and often when the dusty work was done, he invited them back to his nearby house, with its office attached. His wife, Matilda, insisted they stay for supper. By the time they arrived home it was late evening, but what a satisfactory day it had been.

Hi for the hopper and the clanking wheels
And the dunder through the walls ...
Hi for the kiln and the good turf smell
And the corn so crisp and dry. [6]

---

[6] *W. F. Marshall, Omagh. Known as "The Bard of Tyrone"*

CHAPTER VI

Robinson Crusoe and *Cú Chulainn,*
1843

One night William was reading one of his own favourite stories to his wife and father. He had assumed that Polly and Eliza would not be interested. So absorbing was the tale that he did not notice two small figures wrapped in blankets creeping down the stairs to listen.

William came to the moment when Robinson Crusoe, shipwrecked and alone on his desert island, suddenly sees a large footprint in the sand. An enormous footprint! There was a gasp of horror from the hitherto silent figures on the steep staircase. Two small voices said in unison, "Go on, do go on, don't stop! What happens next?"

Then and there William discovered that his new daughters eminently preferred tales of adventure to the pallid stuff the Kildare

Society thought fit to provide for the girls at their village school, which Polly, aged six, now attended with Eliza, along with about a dozen other children.

"Didn't you ever want to run away to sea?" they asked breathlessly. Of course he did, but his mother Molly wasn't very well, and he wasn't about to break her heart as Crusoe did. And Crusoe had toiled for months on end to create a tiny farm there in the middle of his ocean, when William had all that land right at his feet. Nevertheless, he had often gone to the house in Dromore where the surgeon Dr. W. lived, to listen to his enthralling tales of life at sea on a man-of-war. Until one day Dr. W. pulled a knife on him in a drunken fit.

Thereafter, William took to reading tales of adventure around the fire at night until bedtime, while Jane knitted quietly in the shadows of the great chimney. Even Mrs. McAlistair professed to be enthralled, supplying a suitable chorus of, "You don't say! Fancy that," at the most exciting moments.

After the adventures of Robinson Crusoe, William decided to try out a famous Ulster story, *The Cattle Raid of Cooley*. He assumed that Polly would empathize with the fierce Queen Maebh of Connaught who wanted the giant Ulster Bull at all costs. Little did he realize that the descriptions of the young Cú Chulainn would also register with at least one of his young listeners.

Beautiful indeed was the youth who thus came to display his form to the hosts, namely Cú Chulainn mac Sualtain. He seemed to have three kinds of hair, dark next to his skin, blood-red in the middle and hair like a crown of gold covering them outside. Fair was the arrangement of that hair with three coils in the hollow in the nape of his neck, and like gold thread was each fine hair, loose-flowing, bright-golden, excellent, long-tressed, splendid and of beautiful colour, which fell back over his shoulders. A hundred bright crimson ringlets of flaming red-gold encircled his neck. Around his head a hundred strings interspersed with carbuncle-gems ...

All well and good, but this same youth could also terrify his enemies in a way that would serve Polly well at a later date.

In the meantime, Polly would catch a brief glimpse of the famous bull itself, thanks to her sister. Early one morning Polly wakened to hear Eliza calling her to hurry. And hurry she did, getting all tangled up in the sleeves of her shift. By the time she had scampered down from the loft, Eliza was already out the front door.

And there on the crest of the stony outcropping behind the house was an amazing four-legged creature, its horns outlined by a fiery ring of palest gold, half-visible against the darker part of the sky as the mist swirled around it. Both children stood in awe of this creature out of legend.

And then William came around the corner with a pail of feed, and the creature raised its head and gave out an enormous friendly bawl of greeting. Polly stifled a giggle. But she would always remember the magical bull of Ulster as she glimpsed it that morning. And the stories of the four-year-old warrior Cú Chulainn would yet come to her aid.

August brought the birth of little Maggie, so christened after her Drumquin cousin Margaret. Young Joseph was immensely pleased to have a smaller creature than himself to tease. August also brought the arrival of Polly's nemesis, her cousin Matthew Fleming. His father had decided that Joseph's calming influence might have a beneficial effect on this spoiled son of his, and had asked if the lad might help with the harvest.

Polly gleefully pictured him up to his armpits in the reeking flax dam, but what on earth was she to do in the meantime? The trouble had begun the year before on his first visit to the farm with his family. She had entered into the excitement of preparations, the sweeping, dusting, baking, plucking and cooking. The bedding had all been laid out on the bushes.

Then came the clatter of hooves, men dismounting, sweet-faced Mrs. Fleming giving her a hug. Then this tall youth with tow hair, in an immaculate white linen shirt and spotless britches, who had towered over her, saying carelessly, "Ah, Polly, no doubt named after the little cow with no horns, the little *porleagh* creature is it?" Then unaware of the mortal wound he had just inflicted, he had moved away for more interesting adult conversation.

Little *porleagh* cow, indeed. I will never, ever forgive him, Polly swore to herself. The light over Bridgewater Farm had dimmed, and that night Polly pummeled her pillow in frustration.

Now she couldn't believe he was coming to stay for three whole months. How would she ever survive when just the very sight of him with his snooty airs made her see red. She could picture herself dying tragically, possibly of apoplexy, and then he would be sorry.

He might well be, Eliza pointed out, but then Polly wouldn't be there to see it. What was she to do?

There would be no adult sympathy. You were expected to deal with your troubles as best you could. It was going to be a miserable three months. Joseph wondered how Polly would cope, as he observed the small thundercloud sitting at his table.

Spring turned into summer and the Carnalea Flemings arrived to deposit their son. True to form, Matthew once again looked down his nose and drawled lazily, "Why, hello little Polly cousin," and added just under his breath, "Hello, adorable little *porleagh* creature, or are we growing horns now?"

Polly was ready for him. Drawing herself up to her full height which brought her just about opposite his chest, she tilted her chin, looked him straight in the eye, smiled sweetly, and said, "Why hello Freckles Fleming, how delightful to have you come and stay with us." Joseph nearly choked when he saw the look of alarm spread slowly over the young man's face, a face which was indeed covered with a generous sprinkling of freckles, no doubt to the dismay of its owner. It is going to be an interesting three months, Joseph thought. Polly was not finished, however.

"I understand from listening to farmers around here that a short-horned cow is a *moile* cow, not a *porleagh* cow as you called it," she said, pronouncing every word carefully. "And our great friend Mr. Slevin roared with laughter when I told him about your 'porleagh' cow. 'There is no such word in the Irish language, as far as I know.' he said, and he should know. So perhaps you'd better brush up on your vocabulary," she finished, stumbling just for a fraction of a second on the last word.

Joseph listened to all this with a great deal of hidden amusement. Polly had indeed found a valuable ally, one of a family of local schoolmasters known as the Latiner Slevins, who all lived in the parish of Dromore. Arthur Slevin often stopped by of an evening. Joseph had known him for years. He could tell ghost stories that would make your hair stand on end. Sometimes he would bring a battered guitar, and as neighbours dropped by after the day's work, each would sing one of the old songs handed down for generations, many of them never written down. Arthur Slevin could speak Greek and Latin as well as Irish and English, and until recently had taught sixty pupils in a sod cabin built to replace one of the famous hedge-schools. These had sprung up when Catholics were not allowed their own education and were at first hidden away. There were at least fifteen of these schools in Dromore Parish alone.

Polly's own school was located in a small thatched cottage at the foot of Church Street in Dromore. There were never more than twelve pupils attending at any given time, according to its early records, about five of them Church of Ireland, three Presbyterian and four Roman Catholic. It was run on rather strict lines, and Polly and Eliza always thought the hedge schools with forty to sixty pupils sounded like much more fun, especially with teachers like the Slevins, and Patrick Starr in Meldrum.

As the summer continued, Matthew at first weighed in with all kinds of advice about the newest methods of farming, then discovered that Joseph and William had already heard them all, discarded some, and adopted the few that were useful for the heavy clay soil of the farm.

Matthew made a few attempts to pull Polly's hair. A few protesting frogs were thrust down her back. It was such fun to tease someone who turned so red in the face. Then one day he had the scare of his life. Before his eyes the tiny young girl became an enraged creature, so fierce of aspect, with hair standing on end and eyes nearly rolling in the back of her head, that he fled back to the house to report that his cousin had gone quite mad. Of course, he had never heard the story of the young Cú Chulainn, but Mrs. McAlistair had, and thereafter both Polly and Eliza were banished for days from story time. Jane just smiled when she saw two small figures in blankets perched on the staircase to the loft, but she made Polly promise never to roll her eyes back like that again. To add veracity to her portrayal of the young Ulster hero, Polly had cut her hair with some blunt instrument, but it grew in by the end of the summer.

When she and Eliza were helping their mother pull the flax, Matt as they now called him, grudgingly offered to help, muttering, "Women's work," as it usually was. But to everyone's surprise when it came to the heavier work of drowning, retting, heaving and drying the flax, he was in there with the best of them, standing up to his waist in the stinking pond on the other side of the coach road. William loaned him an old shirt. By evening it could practically stand up by itself, he swore, but he kept at it.

When it was time to bring in the oats that September, Matthew pulled his weight. He clearly enjoyed the company of the other men, as they sang to get through the heaviest part of the work, moving in rhythm, one field at a time, going from one farm to the next in turn. He proved adept at the painstaking task of tying the corn sheaves with a spancel. It is easier to take orders from someone other than your own father, Joseph thought wryly. He often remembered a story he had heard from a Rathlin Island man with five brothers. When the eldest refused point blank to obey an order from his father, he beat the living daylights out of him. Thereafter, there was no trouble. Not a method he recommended, but there were times when he had been tempted.

It was quite clear that Polly had never forgiven her cousin. She was polite but frosty. It was a tempest in a very small teapot. That autumn there were far weightier concerns around every hearth.

1843 had been declared 'Repeal Year' by Daniel O'Connell, a time to undo the act of Union and give Ireland back its own parliament. People in the three southern provinces had turned out by the thousands to hear 'The Liberator'. Whether you agreed or disagreed with his policies, no one could ignore the member for Clare. They said the mad old King George had thrown down his pen in a fit of rage when asked to sign the paper admitting O'Connell to the House of Commons in England. Perhaps a million people would be going to the largest gathering of all at Clontarf. Then, abruptly, the meeting was banned, O'Connell arrested and thrown into prison. No one could foresee the consequences.

Meanwhile, Commissioners for the Devon Report listened to descriptions of farming conditions across Ireland from farmers, magistrates, agents, and clergy. Joseph and William didn't need to be told how serious the situation was, even though the North with tenant rights was in marginally better shape. Farmers were unable to sell their produce for enough money to cover rents that had doubled in thirty years. All kinds of good suggestions were made for improving conditions, but none of them addressed the underlying causes of a situation reeling inexorably out of control.

The majority of the farmers did not own their own land. Middlemen made a living from a ruthless extraction of the last cent from tenants already deep in debt. The Irish were known for their strength and height. A man could survive well on a diet of fifteen pounds of potatoes a day and buttermilk, a woman on perhaps twelve pounds. But the experts were worried about the dependence on this one crop. The majority of farms across Ireland were five acres or even less.

In the nearby town of Omagh the markets were booming, but on the sidelines were a growing number of labourers who could find little or no work. Farmers could not afford to employ them, and still pay the exorbitant rent.

CHAPTER VII

A Day to Remember, 1844

"What is he up to now, I wonder?" muttered William Fleming to himself. His father Joseph had gotten up unusually early on this chilly November day. He had milked the cows, scrubbed his face, hands and beard in the cold spring water from the barrel, then dusted off the old jacket he refused to replace, and downed his porridge with scarcely a word except something vague about "the price of oats in Omagh."

It wasn't even market day, yet there was a sack of their best oats already slung up on the cart in the yard with Bluebell the mare hitched up and raring to go.

"Oh Grampa, let me come with you," begged Polly, who felt in her bones something interesting was about to happen. "I've never been to Omagh except once in my entire whole life, so long ago I can hardly remember."

All seven years of your entire whole life, thought Jane wryly as she was just about to say a firm: No, go and do your chores. Then she saw the look in her daughter's eyes. She remembered a time in her own childhood when she had been forbidden to go on a special trip to Enniskillen with her Grampa Fair. Two months later he was dead of pneumonia. Ignoring Mrs. McAlistair's disapproving sniff, she helped Polly into her warmest long wool skirt and bright plaid scarf, tossed some bread and cheese into a handkerchief and waved the two of them off with a stern injunction to be home before dusk.

As the mare turned her head at the Omagh road, Polly could sense her grandfather's energy rising. Something important was going to happen and he was going to be there. Soon she could glimpse the golden colours of autumn trees begin to appear and disappear through the early morning mists.

After nine long plodding miles, the rooftops of Omagh began to appear in the distance against the cloud-covered blue slopes of the Sperrin Mountains. The first sight of the town had always given Joseph a lift. Now he began to tell Polly stories she had never heard before about the days he had worked there as a young stonemason on the building of the great courthouse. There it was, rising majestically at the top of High Street, not far from the very spot where the castle of the O'Neills had reigned supreme so many years before.

Joseph remembered the fury of the architect when one of the huge carved stones for the portico had cracked in two as it was being transported from the far distant quarry, delaying the opening. He, as the youngest of the masons, had been sent post-haste to find a replacement. It was a proud day indeed when he saw the last of the huge Doric columns finally lifted into place in that year of 1822.

"Now you're going to meet one of the people I knew then when he was a rambunctious youngster, so full of energy he was always in trouble. Now he's considered to be one of the town's most respected merchants and entrepreneurs, and today is a very special day indeed for him."

Joseph left the mare and cart in the care of one of the stable lads at the Royal Arms where he knew the owner. He slung the big bag of oats as easily over his shoulder as though it were full of feathers, then ambled up High Street with Polly at his side. "Here we are," he said as he turned in at a big sign marked: *PRINTING ESTABLISHMENT: John Nelis proprietor.* "Now we'll find out what my old friend is up to."

Joseph deposited his oats in a corner of the courtyard, then guided Polly toward the unmistakable sounds of clicking, thudding, wheels turning, curses and bustle that announced a printing press in full swing. Polly was soon enveloped in the overpowering smell of wet ink, damp paper and human sweat.

"You're here in the right place at the right time, Joseph," a voice behind them said.

Joseph hardly recognized his friend, usually so dapper and meticulously groomed. John Nelis looked as though he had scarcely slept for a week, as indeed he had not. His clothes were wrinkled, and ink seemed to have landed randomly over his entire person, even on tufts of his hair.

"Forgive my hair standing on end," he said as he waved a page of newsprint at them. "I've just about been tearing it out." Polly looked at him with immediate interest. She had never heard a grown-up admit to such a thing before.

"Look at the poor quality of paper that idiot sent me." Nelis grumbled on. "The ink sinks right into it. You can hardly read a word. Here see for yourself," he said as he thrust a copy into Joseph's hands, a tell-tale gleam of satisfaction in his eye.

It has long been a matter of astonishment, Joseph read out loud as though to an imaginary audience, *that a county of such extent and importance as the county of Tyrone ... —* "Why, John I can read every word, and I tell you it has a great ring to it."

Warming to his task, he continued, *A district which has manifested, within the last few years, evident signs on the part of its widely increasing population of agriculture and commercial improvement, and which at present exhibits the good results arising from the efforts of its inhabitants ... to turn to the best account its great natural capabilities ... should be without a special organ in the press, to represent its wants, wishes and opinions ...*

The press had stopped for a moment and in the lull their voices carried.

And here we come forward, conscious of none other than the best motives and intentions to supply the long felt and regretted want, chimed in a young voice full of laughter.

"I know the whole thing just about by heart, having set it letter by letter. You should have seen my esteemed brother pacing the floor night before last, reading out his masterpiece to us, as we all chipped in a phrase or two."

"This is young Oliver McCutcheon,[7] our best reporter and brother of James McCutcheon, our editor," broke in John Nelis hastily, deciding to overlook this impertinent interruption on the part of an eighteen-year-old whose enthusiasm had fired up the young typesetters through the long tedious hours of standing required to proof and set the entire four pages of the paper letter by letter, word by word, making sure not to mix up the different sizes of type.

"See for yourself, young Miss," said Oliver, gravely handing Polly a copy of the paper. It was still slightly damp, so she held it gingerly away from her apron, looking for an easy phrase to read. There it was, *OMAGH, FRIDAY, NOVEMBER 8, 1844* – a day she would remember for a long time. Hastily she turned the page, hoping for more words that she could as easily decipher. Never had the importance of being able to read properly so impressed itself upon her. All kinds of possibilities could open up if you were able to understand all these words set down in front of you. Now there was a word that leaped out at her from page three. It had been on last week's spelling test at school. *RAILWAY*, it said in bold letters. "Are we really going to have our own railway line at long last?" she asked in astonishment. "All my school friends are talking about it — we all are dying to ride on it, but we'd just about given up hope it would come our way."

---

[7] *At a later date this young man would leave journalism to become one of the well-known preachers of his day*

"Yes, the railway is indeed on its way in our direction," replied John Nelis with all the gravity he might have accorded one of the town fathers. "Yes it is, and your postmaster in Dromore, John McLaughlin, will soon be asked to put up a public notice of the plans."

Then and there, Polly decided that one way or another she would ride on that train. And John Nelis most certainly was someone you never forgot, once you had met him. Little wonder he was easily elected as a member of Omagh's first Town Commissioners the next year. And he had the most interesting array of things to sell at his printing establishment (well-advertised in a right-hand column in that first issue).

Joseph decided it was time to get down to business. He coughed gently. "Would you take a bag of the very best oats in exchange for one of your papers? As you know hard cash is scarce these days," he inquired, in the tones in which all such matters were conducted at local fairs.

John Nelis roared with laughter. He knew down to the last penny what oats would fetch at the market the next day. He'd just set a column listing all the market prices, one of the many services his paper would provide for local farmers.

"Those oats of yours are worth half a dozen of these papers, truth to tell, if it weren't for that cursed stamp tax the Government has imposed. Almost a day's wage for a labourer. I tell you that tax will cut our circulation by at least half. In the meantime, though, I'll trade you two papers for that sack of yours. Just this once, mind you, as a notable exception," he added hastily, envisaging mountains of oats piling up at his office.

And so it was that Joseph Fleming became the proud owner of two of the very first copies of the *Tyrone Constitution*. "You've got a winner, John," he murmured quietly, as they watched the young apprentices loading bales of newsprint onto the carts waiting to transport them to Fintona, Ballygawley and all the other nearby towns. The daily mail coaches would take other bales to Dublin and Londonderry.

And a winner it proved to be. Within a short time *The World*, a prominent English publication at the time, would comment: *It is a very promising newspaper both as regards matter and topography. A local paper was, we think, much required in the district, and we are sure, judging from the gentleman who controls the* Tyrone Constitution *that it will be conducted with tact and ability.*

After a brief stop at William M'Feeters bakery for a freshly-baked bun, Joseph and Polly went exploring, past Gallows Hill and the gloomy old Gaol with the Lunatic Asylum attached, and on to the bright relief of the Butter Market where women were already preparing for the Saturday sale.

All along the lively back streets of Omagh, small shops with thatched roofs clung to the steep slopes, crowded in among taller buildings crowned with slate roofs. There were saddles and harness-makers, tailors and tallow chandlers, spade and shovel makers, woollen drapers, and watch and clock makers, and Lusk's Mercantile Ink.

Mr. Kiernan offered hardware, ironmongery and groceries all in one place. Smaller groceries could be found on nearly every corner, so many of them (eighteen in all) that Polly ran out of fingers trying to count them. One of them belonged to John Caldwell, a distant cousin of her mother, Polly discovered, albeit about five times removed. Really, you might well find some connection with just about everyone you met, if not to your own family then at least to someone you knew.

There was her grandfather, just now talking to George Buchanan, Chief Distributor of Stamps for the whole of County Tyrone, whom he knew because the Buchanans, a distinguished Omagh family, were related to the Sproules, and Sarah Sproule had married young James Dill, the Presbyterian minister from Dromore.

"Have you seen our new paper?" George Buchanan was asking her grandfather, waving a copy under his nose.

"Yes, yes, and it is all your fault, with those stamps of yours, that it's costing us such a pretty penny," Joseph retorted. "Now tell me how your father is doing?" James Buchanan had just retired as British Consul in New York and was widely respected for his advocacy of free trade, knowledge of the native people, and forward-looking approach to public policy.

Joseph was also interested to learn that George's nephew, Alexander Carlisle Buchanan, was working hard as Chief Immigration Agent for the Port of Québec, and was sending home enthusiastic reports of farmland for purchase in the Province of Canada. As Polly listened to the two men talking, she could not have imagined that less than three years later this same Buchanan nephew would play a decisive role in saving countless Irish lives, including her own. Still listening with half an ear to their talk, she drifted a few yards down the street, and stopped suddenly, rooted to the spot.

There in the tiny front window of the smallest shop you ever saw was a single hat. It was made of fine straw, wound around several times with elegant mauve ribbon, tied with a large bow in the back. Over the windows was a sign that read, *Rebecca and Mary Wright, Milliners.*

Joseph coughed gently to get her attention, then hurried them both down the street. He was not about to encourage such extravagance. At that moment, however, Polly made up her mind that one day she would wear a hat like that. Meanwhile she followed Joseph as he strolled down to the Campsie Bridge where an older man was patiently fishing, despite the lateness of the season. Nearby was the dramatic convergence of the Camowen and Drumragh Rivers with the Strule.

Tired and happy, Polly nodded off as the mare plodded home along the old road from Omagh to Dromore, not knowing that one day a poet, Felix Kearney, would weave those words into a memorable song. Mindful of Jane's injunction, they arrived back at the farm just in the nick of time, before dusk closed in.

Never again in his life would Joseph do anything as wildly extravagant as buying a newspaper at that price, five pence. That evening in November, however, he was in his element. Word spread about his purchase, and soon the hearth room was packed with neighbours who stayed till all hours, reading and rereading sections of the paper out loud for all to admire, and discuss at length.

William drew a good laugh with his exaggerated rendering of the huge ad displayed prominently on the paper's front page. "Listen to this," he declaimed. "The really big news is that there might just be one single cure for all that ails you. *Holloway's ointment will cure anything, Dangerous Wounds, Bad Legs, Bad Breasts, Sore Throats, Yaws, African King's Evil'* — whatever in the world that might be —*'Ulcerated Cancers, Piles, Tremours, Swellings'* and last but not least, your everyday *'Stiff Joints, Chilblains, Gout and even Rheumatism'.*"

Foreign Intelligence carried news from every corner of the world you could possibly want to know about. But Hugh Maguire was more impressed with coverage closer to home. The editor, James McCutcheon, and his paper might disagree strongly with Daniel O'Connell's policies, but they gave the member for Clare generous coverage.

And less than three years after O'Connell's imprisonment, when it was discovered he was indeed seriously ill, the paper's expression of regret had a genuine ring to it.

As she listened to all the talk that evening, Jane was quietly nursing twin babies, Isabella and Rebecca, who had been born on July 11. She found the news of the latest fashions from London quite diverting although she could never afford them. But the paper won her greatest loyalty when it reported the exploit of a young woman named Catharine Woods from Dunmore. At the age of just fifteen, Catharine had spun a linen thread from a few hanks of flax so fine and so strong that it could reach around the entire globe. As a spinner herself, Jane could appreciate the marvel of such an achievement. She had spent many an evening at her wheel, her foot tap-tap-tapping, as the rough shanks of flax turned into an even thread glinting in the firelight.

The next day Joseph took a load of oats and the second copy of the *Con*, as everyone now called the paper, over to his brother Andrew at the mill in Shanmullagh. It was an immediate hit with the farmers there, as he knew it would be. In the following weeks the favour was returned. One way or another everyone kept up with the latest news, even the election of a new American President, the unknown James Polk from Donegal and Tennessee. The quality of newsprint improved dramatically, circulation doubled and eventually the hated stamp tax was lifted. The price of the paper would drop to an affordable one pence.

CHAPTER VIII

Polly and her Teacher

When Eliza and Polly finally made their way home through the driving sleet of a dark November day, Grandpa Fleming was there as usual in his chair, as close to the fire as he could manage without getting in the way of the womenfolk.

"How was school?" he asked, as he always did.

"It was terrible," wailed Polly as she pulled off her wet overcoat. "I couldn't seem to spell anything properly. The harder I tried the more trouble I was in. That awful new replacement teacher, Mrs. Finch, rapped me across the knuckles so hard I dropped my pencil on the floor. And what good does that do, I'd like to know? The mean old cow," she added almost under her breath. But Joseph had sharp ears. He looked sternly at his new grandchild, hiding the twinkle that would otherwise betray him.

"That is no way to talk about your teacher, young woman. And if you would spend a little more time at your lessons, and a little less up that tree of yours, you might find spelling not as hard as you think. By tomorrow night I want you to tell me how to spell 'ambidextrous.' And let's see if you can learn to spell 'sparbled,' as in 'take off those sparbled boots when you walk on my clean floor,' as my wife Molly used to say to me."

"Is that a real word?" Jane asked. "I had never heard it before I came here."

"Of course it is," replied Joseph, somewhat tartly. "It's what we've always called our work boots, and in my view it's a much more interesting word than hob-nailed, as the rest of you describe them." Polly agreed thoroughly and added this word to others like 'spancel' and 'scutch' that made everyday life that much more vivid by their use. However, her grandfather was not finished. "And Albert," he said to the young hired lad who had come to help him that year, "would you just run over to Mrs. Finch's and ask her to be kind enough to come by here at her leisure."

Polly stared at her grandfather, appalled. What on earth was he up to now? No hint showed on his weather-beaten old face. An hour later, Mrs. Finch could be seen striding up the lane. Polly's heart sank.

After the usual polite enquiries, mutually exchanged, about the state of one's health, the crops this year, and the new school board, Joseph said to Mrs. Finch, "This afternoon my granddaughter made a very interesting remark about you, and I thought perhaps she might like to say it directly to you." Polly was stunned; if she could have sunk through the floor right then and there, she would gladly have done so.

"Why, Mrs. Finch," she finally stammered with as much poise as she could muster, "I do believe Grandfather must mean the sentiment I expressed earlier that you are an exemplary example of the milk of human kindness, in spending your valuable days dealing with such intractable pupils as myself." Polly was throwing in as many long words as she could muster, most of them picked up from listening to her elders talking of an evening.

"I also recognize, Mrs. Finch, that it is easier for me to appreciate the beauty of a tree when I am up in it than it is to know how to spell 'deciduous,' but I am resolved to try to improve. And I do know how to spell 'SCUTCH.' It's one of my very favourite words. You can just hear the whack and thump of it when you say it."

"Very nicely said, Polly," said Mrs. Finch with a glance at Joseph, "I appreciate the import of your remark," and she added, as she took her leave, "I'm not sure that I was quite so complimentary to my teacher when I was your age, especially when I was perched out of sight in my favourite tree. Will that be all, Joseph?" she asked with a knowing look at the old man. "If so, I'll be on my way. And by the way, Polly, by tomorrow I will expect you to at least know how to spell 'apple' properly. 'APPUL' will definitely not do! And if it's not asking too much, 'turnip' as well. And it would help," she said to no one in particular, but with some asperity, "if the Flemings could make up their minds whether we're to use one or two m's in spelling their family name. This habit of our people spelling their names one way on Tuesday and another on Wednesday is most confusing."

"School-marm to the core," muttered Joseph as Mrs. Finch made a dignified exit after this parting shot. "But don't you ever forget, Polly, what you've learned tonight. Never say anything behind someone's back that you are unwilling to say right to their face."

Mr. Lendrum, the regular schoolmaster, was due back in the fall. Polly and her teacher managed to get through the remaining weeks of the school year. As spring progressed, Mrs. Finch decided to take the children on walks in the countryside, pointing out the amazing variety of trees and plants around them.

In olden times the Druids used to make wands from ash branches, she told them, and ash trees and witches were closely associated. Ash also means a safe spot. You could stand in the shadow of an ash tree to avoid mischievous fairy spirits.

Polly decided to try this next time her archenemy Freckles came around. Her mother had already placed warm ash sap in her ear that awful time she had an earache. She wished that there were a beech tree right on the farm, because Mrs. Finch told them that you could say a prayer under it, and the prayer would go straight to heaven. Polly wondered if that might possibly help to remove Freckles as rapidly as possible from her vicinity.

It might also be very important some day to know that if one of the children was taken by fairies, you could make a fire of blackthorn on the peak of a fairy hill, and the child would be returned to you. Polly was less pleased to discover that you had to beware of walking through a bluebell wood, for it can be a place of concentrated fairy magic and enchantment. Only once in her life had she ever seen such a wood, and she had always hoped to return to it. It was a relief to discover that the cowslips she and Eliza picked early that spring were an invaluable fairy flower. Her mother had made cowslip wine as a cure for headache. Jane always claimed it helped her memory and restored youthful blossom and beauty. She also made dandelion tea as a spring tonic. Just drinking it made you feel good. There were all kinds of other wonderful things that Polly learned on those spring walks with Mrs. Finch. She hadn't known that an elder tree was a good place to take shelter in a storm. It would never be struck by lightning because it was the tree of the Cross. And you must always remember that if you use an elder for shelter, you should ask the tree's permission.

One of the highlights of Polly's week was the Saturday trip into Dromore with her mother to buy cotton thread or candles and to barter eggs for tea and sugar. The main thoroughfare, Church Street, wasn't all that large, but it was full of interest, with the brightly painted shop fronts, and the house of the Stewart family who had been in Dromore as long as anyone could remember and had most likely founded the town. There you passed William Guy's Shop, now run by his son, and the homes of James Price and Andrew Hamilton. There was no stop at the blacksmith's, which annoyed Polly immensely. Only William or Joseph were allowed in there. It was an exclusive men's club, where opinions and gossip were exchanged and such news as could be considered too important for women's ears.

As far as Polly was concerned, the smithy was the most interesting place in the village. Perhaps I'll be a blacksmith when I grow up, she thought to herself, then I'll invite all my friends, and men will have to ask very politely to be allowed to enter.

CHAPTER IX

Crisis Approaches, 1845

On April 20 that year the entire Fleming family and their near neighbours trooped up to the church on the Brae for the wedding of Jane's friend, Catherine Hamilton. Catherine was the daughter of Patrick Hamilton, farmer and also shoemaker, on the nearby Lakemount Estate. She was marrying Thomas Little, a farmer from Kilskeery.

The menfolk were outfitted in their freshly starched white linen shirts and nearly new suits. Jane looked stunning in a new muslin dress made for her by Miss Thompson, the Dromore seamstress, with extra material at the waist to hide her latest pregnancy. Polly and Eliza placed young Joseph between them in the old pew, with a twin on each of their laps

After Benjamin Marshall pronounced Catherine and Thomas man and wife, he paused for a moment. "This could well be one of the last weddings we will celebrate in this church," he said slowly.

"Soon the new church will be ready and this one will stand empty, open to the wind and rain. But never forget, it is still a sacred place. People have prayed on this spot since the time of St. Patrick." And with that William Henry, the organist, did his best with the organ's rusty old pipes and they all trooped out to a fine feast laid out on wooden trestles at the nearby Lakemount Estate.

That summer people in Omagh were in a good mood. The harvest promised to be plentiful. The Diamond, a favourite meeting place behind the Courthouse, was thronged with an unusual number of citizens. Railway fever was spreading and half the landed proprietors and merchants of the town were hurrying along to snap up the last shares of the brand new Omagh and Armagh Railway.

John Nelis was of course in his element in all this bustle, as founder of the newspaper that could provide you with the latest news from far and near. One of the regular visitors to his office was especially interested in railway news. Young James Brown came by to Omagh each month to take orders for the fine quality soap and candles produced at his family's factory in Donaghmore. This was the soap everyone, Jane included, depended upon for the great Monday wash-days, omission of which would cause one's hygiene and even one's honour to be called into question.

James had left school at fourteen to join the firm on the death of his father. He had worked long hours with his brother, unloading the creels full of kelp brought mainly by canal all the way from the west coast of Donegal. The green weeds that still smelled of the sea were an essential ingredient in the making of soap.

Now at the mature age of twenty-two, James liked nothing better than to travel far and wide through Tyrone, Fermanagh and parts of Derry and Armagh, driving his own horse and gig and taking down orders.

John Nelis enjoyed the visits of this young entrepreneur who among other talents was a good storyteller. He had many tales to tell about his father who had braved the dangers of highwaymen. He was not always the victor in these skirmishes in those earlier days as a linen merchant, making the long three-day journey to Dublin on horseback.

David Brown was always on good terms with his Catholic neighbours. On one occasion when the weather looked threatening, the local priest, Friar Conwell, gave him the use of his chapel as a temporary store for his corn. However, a funeral had to take place before Brown could take advantage of his offer. Out the back door went the corn.

As the sky became more and more overcast, the priest paced up and down. Finally, he strode out of the church and up to the top of the hill overlooking the road by which the funeral procession must come. "At last, he came back to my father," James recounted, "and announced, 'Here they are, coming as if they were on their way to the gallows'." The priest saw to it that the funeral was held at a brisk pace and the corn was whisked into the chapel in the nick of time just before the heavens opened.

James Brown was just fifteen at the time of the 'Big Wind'. He remembered the roof coming off the brewery coolers that

Bridgewater Farm on the left side of the old coach road.

held the famous Donaghmore ale. One of the workmen, George Mulholland, sauntered casually in the next morning, cool as a cucumber. When asked how he had put in the night – knowing he had a thatched cottage that could have gone up in flames – "Oh, all right," said he quite calmly, "I just slept on the roof to keep it on."

In October that year, young James Brown came to Omagh as usual. This time he had a very different story to tell.

"Early in the month I had inspected the back field of potatoes owned by our family. The crop promised to be a good one this year. Then, in a single night, the plants were struck with the blight and both tops and roots blackened."

"Because the crop was almost matured, part of the plants could be salvaged for food. The rest went to feed the pigs or to make starch. I and my brother installed a small machine to grind the potatoes and extract the flour. And for this purpose they still served very well."

John Nelis listened intently. He and his editor James McCullough made sure their readers benefitted from any solution that could save even part of the potato crop. The experts disagreed. No one knew the cause of the blight. People hoped that next year's crop would be better. The government, maintaining the crisis was temporary, delayed action even while people in the south and west of Ireland were starving. John Nelis was concerned. Already on August 29 his paper had carried an ominous warning.

A fatal malady has broken out among the potato crop and destruction is everywhere.

By November everyone knew that half the potato crop had been lost to this malady. In the midst of all the anxiety, Jane had given birth to her seventh child, their second son, whom they promptly named Robert. William and his father did their best to keep the worst of the news away from Jane, but it was no use. Mrs. McAlistair could never resist being the first to bear bad tidings. "The *Con* is saying," she trumpeted, "that the oat crop alone could feed twice our population. Yet each week sixteen thousand quarters of oats are being shipped out of the country. What are we to do, what with all the rents and taxes to pay? There'll be no good end to it."

Meantime, on December 23, just at Christmastime, a letter was received from the Poor Law Commissioners at Dublin ordering a cutback in the food served at the nearby workhouse in Lowtherstown. No one, not even child, was to be given supper. Jane was horrified. What if those were my children? she thought.

Sparbled boots.

CHAPTER X

News Spreads like Wildfire, 1846

Since early January, the Church of Ireland rector, Henry Lucas St. George, had continued to receive distressing news from his family in Kilkenny. Throughout the south of Ireland, hunger was widespread. Towards the end of January heavy rains were raising the fears of everyone. And yet the nature of this blight continued to puzzle the experts. One field had been affected, while the one right next to it remained whole.

The Permanent Secretary of the Treasury, Charles Trevelyan, in faraway Whitehall was setting his cautious, penny-pinching mark on the relief effort. Seven hundred relief committees were only now being established in Ireland. *Minute reports of circumstances of each family from whom application for relief may be made* would be demanded of them. Only a few of these committees were in the North, none in Tyrone. There was still hope that Ulster might escape the worst of the blight.

On August 8, Joseph went up to Lakemount House as usual to sell some of the extra vegetables. He found the household strangely silent. One of the young maids had obviously been weeping. Major Hamilton was just coming out of his study with the foreman, both of them looking grim. They stopped when they saw Joseph, and the Major told him, "Young James Brown from Donaghmore has just come by with some terrible news. He drove with his sister Isabella to Bundoran on the third. On the way there the potato fields were in full flower. On their way back yesterday morning, those same crops were blackened and useless, with a horrible smell rising from the fields themselves. James is not an easy man to rattle, but I've never seen him so worried."

A few days later, on August 20, Subconstable Montgomery of the Lowtherstown Constabulary wrote to his superior ...*Regret to say that the disease in the potato crops in this union has appeared to an alarming extent and to all appearances threatens to be most destructive.* The news spread like wildfire. Then on August 28, the British government prorogued until January, sending its sitting members home, with the clear intent of shifting the whole problem onto the Irish landlords, and local relief committees.

By the end of the year, in spite of all the local efforts, the situation was out of control.

The Tuesday, December 8th issue of the **Northern Whig** described the alarming onset of fever, of a type classed by the physicians as famine-fever, which afflicted hundreds of the poor; and dysentery as well, produced by cold and want of nutritious food. It quoted a

Dr. Donovan from Skibbereen, represented as a most respectable physician.

That morning, he had been followed by a crowd of applicants, looking for coffins for their deceased friends. He had just visited a house in the Windmill, where he saw two dead bodies, awaiting some means of burial. One was that of a girl eleven years of age, who had died from starvation, and the other of a child, the body of which was nearly decomposed. He had no doubt, if measures of the most active nature were not promptly taken to avert it, that they were on the eve of a pestilence, which would reach the higher classes, in fact, every class in society. He entreated them to give him some aid to have these creatures buried.

The Saturday before, *The Whig* had criticized the public works programme, saying, *Two-fifths of the whole expenditure has never found its way into the hands of the working people, but has been swallowed up in salaries to a staff of officers.*

Everyone knew the story of the poor man who had worked on the roads, gone three weeks without a penny in wages, and been found dead, his stomach found empty of food.

December

All through those months, Jane worked tirelessly with the other mothers of the village to collect food for those in most need. John McLaughlin, the postmaster, set up a cauldron on the main street of Dromore to feed the hungry. The local landlords in this area, unlike some others, were generous in their support, but these local efforts were hampered by the unbelievable red tape and parsimonious policies emanating from Trevelyan at faraway London's Treasury Board.

James Reid Dill, the Presbyterian minister, was appointed secretary of the Dromore relief committee, and worked closely with the other clergy and lay people. Thousands passed through their hands in that cold winter. Andrew Fleming continued to grind corn at his Shanmullagh mill, but this time it was Indian corn from America that required twice grinding and produced a meal that was half as nutritious as oat meal, a staple that was still being exported out of the country by the cartload.

One winter night, James Dill rode up to the Fleming's home. He came in covered with snow, exhausted, to sit by the fire for a few moments. "I can't believe what is happening."

"Even though all the churches are working together we are unable to reach everybody. It's a dreadful time. One poor woman from our village was seen just the other night wheeling her dead child in a box-barrow to the graveyard on the Brae where, with her own hands, she buried it as best she could in the falling snow. Our young Catholic curate is at death's door from exhaustion and fever. I fear he won't last long." James Dill stood up now, put on his coat, and turned to make the point he had really come about.

"Jane, you must not go about any longer, and you must now turn away strangers from your door, hard as that may seem" and, as she tried to protest, he added more firmly, "You have eight children to feed and protect; that babe in your arms is your first responsibility.

The fever is rampant everywhere, and now we're finding cases of smallpox and dysentery as well. It's not going to help everyone if you and your household come down too." And with that he turned and went back out into the winter night.

EMPLOYMENT OF THE POOR.

BY THE
LORD LIEUTENANT GENERAL AND GENERAL GOVERNOR OF IRELAND BESSBOROUGH.

WHEREAS, by an Act passed in the tenth year of the reign of her present Majesty, intituled "an act to facilitate the employment of the labouring poor for a limited period in distressed districts in Ireland," it is enacted, that whenever, on representation of the existence of distress in any district, it may seem expedient to the Lord Lieutenant or other Chief Governor or Governors of Ireland, that an Extraordinary Presentment sessions for any Barony, Half-Barony, county of a city, or county of a town in Ireland, (the county of the city of Dublin excepted,) should assemble and make Presentments for the execution of Public Works in such district, it shall be lawful for the Lord Lieutenant or other Chief Governor or Governors of Ireland, from time to time, by a notice to be published in the Dublin Gazette, and also in one or more News-papers circulating in the respective district, and of which notice, copies shall be posted in the usual places for posting public grand jury notices in such district, to direct and require that an Extraordinary Presentment Sessions for each Barony, Half-Barony, county of a city, or county of a town, as the case may be, shall meet and assemble for the purposes of the said act:

And whereas representations have been made to me of the existence of distress in the BARONY of CLOGHER, in the County of Tyrone :

Now, I, JOHN WILLIAM Earl of BESSBOROUGH, Lord Lieutenant General and General Governor of Ireland, do, by this Notice, direct and require that an EXTRAORDINARY PRESENTMENT SESSIONS for the said BARONY of CLOGHER, in the County of Tyrone, shall meet and assemble for the purposes of the said act, at CLOGHER, in the said Barony, on MONDAY, the 12th day of OCTOBER instant, at the hour of TWELVE o'clock at noon.

Dated at Dublin Castle, the 1st day of October, 1846.

By His Excellency's Command
H. LABOUCHERE.

BY THE
LORD LIEUTENANT GENERAL AND GENERAL GOVERNOR OF IRELAND BESSBOROUGH

WHEREAS, by an act passed in the tenth year of the reign of her present Majesty, intituled "an act to facilitate the employment of the labouring poor for a limited period in distressed districts in Ireland," it is enacted, that whenever, on representation of the existence of distress in any district, it may seem expedient to the Lord Lieutenant or other Chief Governor or Governors of Ireland, that an Extraordinary Presentment Sessions for any Barony, Half-Barony, county of a city, or county of a town in Ireland, (the county of the city of Dublin excepted,) should assemble and make Presentments for the execution of Public Works in such district, it shall be lawful for the Lord Lieutenant or other Chief Governor or Governors of Ireland, from time to time, by a notice to be published in the Dublin Gazette, and also in one or more Newspapers circulating in the respective district, and of which notice, copies shall be posted in the usual places for posting public grand jury notices in such district, to direct and require for such Barony, Half Barony, county of a city, or county of a town, as the case may be, shall meet and assemble for the purposes of the said act :

And whereas representations have been made

CHURCH MISSIONARY SOCIETY.

THE ANNUAL SERMON
in aid of this Society, will be preached in OMAGH CHURCH, on SUNDAY, the 11th October, (D.V.) at Noon Service.

W. S. GUTHBERT, Secretary.

Sept. 24, 1846.

TO LET,
FOR A TERM OF YEARS,
Or the Interest in the Lease Sold,

A HOUSE situate in the village of SES-KANORE, County Tyrone, containing 3 Parlours, 6 Bed-rooms, Study, 2 large Gardens, and OUT OFFICES attached, suitable for a Gentleman's family; with FARM adjoining, containing 18½ Irish Acres, being equal to 34 Acres Statute Measure, with right of Turbary. Seskanore is a weekly MARKET TOWN, and a Monthly FAIR has been established, situate within 2 miles of Omagh, and 3 of Beragh, all Post and Market Towns.

For particulars apply to SINCLAIR PERRY, Esq., SESKANORE, TYRONE. All letters must be post paid.

Seskanore, Sept. 21, 1846.

WANTED,
AN APPRENTICE TO THE IRONMONGERY BUSINESS.

Apply to
WILLIAM SCOTT.

Omagh, Oct. 2, 1846

CHURCH EDUCATION SOCIETY.

WANTED,
A MASTER for a SCHOOL, under the above Society, within a short distance of Omagh.

Apply to Rev. J. B. CHAPMAN, Riverland, or Rev. THOMAS LINDSAY STACK, Omagh.

September 24, 1840.

SERVANT MAN WANTED,

A MIDDLE-AGED MAN, without incumbrance, or with only a Wife, who can attend about a House, and understands a little of plain Gardening, will hear of a good permanent situation by applying to the Proprietor of this Paper. He will be required to have good recommendations for honesty and sobriety.

Omagh, Sept. 30, 1846.

Newry, Armagh, and Londonderry Junction Railway Company.

NOTICE IS HEREBY GIVEN, that a first dividend of Ten Shillings per Share will be payable to the SCRIPHOLDERS in this Company, on and after the 23d of September, instant, and for four weeks thereafter, between the hours of Ten and Three o'clock, on application at

The Provincial Bank of Ireland, Dublin, or
The Provincial Bank of Ireland, Newry:

The Scrip presented by each party is to be arranged as nearly as possible in numerical order, and endorsed by the party presenting it : to be left one day for examination, and the payment called for the next day.— The parties will be required to deliver up the Scrip so endorsed, and sign a receipt, and in exchange receive a Certificate, which will entitle them to such further dividend as the Directors may be enabled to pay, after the final settlement of the accounts.

The Directors regret that delays have occurred in the settlement of the accounts of the Company which they did not contemplate ; they have, however, thereby been enabled to make considerable reductions in the accounts, and to satisfy all claims, with the exception of two or three which are still unadjusted.

CLAUD HAMILTON.
F. W. M'BLAIN, Secretary.

10th September, 1846.

Section of *The Tyrone Constitution, Omagh, Friday October 9, 1846.*

CHAPTER XI

Increasing Destitution,
Dromore, December 1846

Two weeks before Christmas, Henry Lucas St. George, the Church of Ireland rector, woke early on a day he had long been working for, the opening of his new church. No longer would his parishioners have to struggle up the hill in the snow to the draughty old church on the Brae, with its leaking roof.

Young Oliver McCutcheon, now just twenty, rode from Omagh in the snow to report for the *Con* of December 18th that some eight hundred people had braved the bitter cold to attend the opening of Dromore's new church. He praised the elegance of both the exterior and the interior with its stained glass windows and candlelit chandeliers purchased by St. George out of his own pocket.

Young Oliver did a praiseworthy job, but an unknown penman from Dromore did him one better.

A single copy of the newspaper, *The Impartial Reporter*, dated Friday, December 18, 1846, was brought by the Caldwell and Fair relatives when they came struggling through the snow to spend Christmas within the hospitable walls of Bridgewater Farm.

Small cousins on three-legged stools crowded around the glowing central hearth fire as Andrew Fleming, the miller from nearby Shanmullagh East, was given the task of reading the latest edition in his stentorian voice so pitched that his words could carry over the rumble of the mill wheel.

A banner headline read:

OPENING OF THE REV. MR. ST. GEORGE'S NEW CHURCH AT DROMORE IN THE CO. TYRONE.

(from a correspondent)
DROMORE, DEC. 12th, 1846.

Dear Sir:

I promised to send you a memorandum of the opening of the church here, which took place yesterday.

In the first place I may mention that the dreadful hurricane which occurred in the year 1839 (Jan. 6th the Big Wind that devastated all Ireland) totally dilapidated the old building.

And yesterday the tempest was so great, and the weather so severe, accompanied by deep snow, that at the early part of the morning we feared it would be almost impossible for any of the families to leave their fireside. However the surrounding neighbours were determined to assemble, being anxious not to disappoint themselves or their venerable and respected Rector who had made such exertions, and undergone such fatigues, added to considerable personal expense to render the building one of the handsomest and most complete in the North, perhaps in the Kingdom of Ireland; and indeed most truly gratified and astonished have I been and consider it one of the happiest days of my life to have had the privilege of being present on that occasion. Indeed I must repeat that it is truly surprising to witness so beautiful a structure dedicated to the King of kings and opened at a moment when the whole country is suffering the horrors of famine, desolation and woes.

The labour and anxiety which it has been necessary for Mr. St.George to use has been amply crowned with success: every part of the building, both externally and internally being complete, the magnificent stained glass window over the communion table, presented by Mr. St. George, and the handsome organ gallery opposite at the end of the aisle, erected at his expense show how great the interest has been which he has taken, and to which he devoted himself almost daily during its erection.

In fact nothing was deficient save the arrival of the organ which had not reached its destination from Dublin.

*Mr. St. George, unfortunately ... laboured under a severe fit of illness, but nothing short of death itself would have prevented him from being at his post. He preached a most excellent sermon from [**St. Matthew ch.19, v. 20**] and was surrounded by an assembly of all sorts, parties and denominations, being held in the highest veneration and respect by every man, rich and poor, who have been acquainted with him. The church was nearly full, although all parties came in covered with* *snow. Families were invited to partake of a splendid dejeuner which was laid out at the Rectory, where many before had frequently partaken of his hospitable entertainment ... his residence is the constant home of presentation of soup and other charities to the sick and destitute.*

Even as Polly marveled at the beauty of this new church, she couldn't help whispering to Eliza that she still missed the old one.

There was something immensely comforting about the old church on the Brae, even just the sight of it, high on its rocky promontory overlooking the town. People had prayed in that location for centuries; you could feel feel it in the walls, damaged as they were. Even after most of the roof had blown off in the Big Wind, people had come here, stumbling among the debris, the young helping the old. In those last terrible months, Catholics and Protestants alike had seen their dead brought on an open cart through the streets of Dromore, up the steep slope to the huge open grave on the slope of the graveyard. Somehow that old church on the Brae now belonged to everyone in a way you couldn't explain. Or so it seemed to Polly and Eliza as they rode silently homeward that day. Joseph had been pressed into service for some of the last minute stonework at the new church. He didn't begrudge the extra labour, but the muscles in his hands and arms were still sore from the cold. It appalled him to think of the men out there working on the roads in this weather to earn enough to feed their families.

Joseph's sense of outrage found an echo in the office of the *Tyrone Constitution* over on High Street where the senior editor, James McCutcheon, was burning the midnight oil. It was Thursday December 17, the paper was due out on the street the following day, and his editorial was not finished. Young Oliver McCutcheon had already helped the typesetters set his own piece about the opening of the new Dromore church. Now he stood by, a willing audience, as his brother James struggled to find words strong enough to wake up the sleeping politicians in Whitehall.

The inadequacy of the government measures of relief to meet the direful calamity which has fallen so heavily upon our unhappy country is each day becoming more fully apparent, James read from his scribbled notes, where words had been crossed out and re-written several times: *The distress of the poor is exhibiting the most painful evidence of rapid increase. On every side blundering incapacity prevails.*

His voice rose a tone, and took on a note of scorn that Oliver had seldom heard from his brother as he took on a target closer to home: *The provision-jobbers are at present realizing immense profits on the food of the starving poor. Enormous profits of up to seventy-five percent scarcely satisfy their rapacity.* He stopped and noted down a final shot: *all due to the chivalrous refusal of a Whig government to interfere with private speculators.*

By now sweat was pouring off his brow, and the oil lamp was beginning to smoke furiously. James McCutcheon had one final word of warning for a faraway Parliament. *Rome itself,* he thundered, *at the height of its power might have trembled at the presence of so disordered and explosive a community. It is not a crisis we are surmounting but a state we have entered.*

In the middle of the following week one of the paper's advertisers came storming into the office of John Nelis, and threw a copy of the

Con on his desk. "If I have to read anymore of this twaddle about the merchant class, I'm going to take my business elsewhere," he bellowed, growing red in the face. "It's Christmas time, and I would have hoped that your paper would take a more cheerful tone. All this bad-mouthing of the government and the rest of us is bad for business."

John Nelis leaned back in his chair, and refrained from commenting that it was indeed Christmas time, and what better time to be talking about the poor. He rather liked this man, in spite of his bluster. He happened to know that the man had in fact contributed to the recent collection for the homeless. "We'll do our best," he said quietly. "You're a valued client. And we've had many a good time together. But future generations won't thank us if we remain silent now, will they? Especially at Christmas," he added, almost under his breath, as the man snorted and turned on his heel to leave.

All week long James McCutcheon wrote and re-wrote his editorial. That Thursday he was still in his office at nine p.m. It was Christmas Eve, and the first year that the Friday publication date coincided with Christmas day. Most of the paper had already been set, and all but one of the typesetters sent home to their families. Oliver McCutcheon had learned enough to set a column if need be. Once again he was on hand to help his brother.

John Nelis stopped by for a moment with some ham and freshly baked bread that he brought from home. "We're right behind you, George," he said as he went on his way back to his office. "Don't pull your punches." He would be there through the night, as the first issues came off the press.

That Christmas day issue arrived at Bridgewater Farm just at suppertime, brought by one of the neighbours who had been in Omagh that day. "Listen to this," said Joseph as his eye caught the first sentence of the editorial:

> "The rapidly increasing destitution of the people, and inadequacy and ineffectual operation of the government measures of relief, form the sole topics of public interest. The distress of the people throughout several parts of the country is absolutely frightful. Famine and fever are doing their deadly work, and the columns of our southern contemporaries are filled with soul-harrowing details of scenes of indescribable misery, sickness, want, and death. Families lying huddled together in empty hovels, naked and starving, are dying, one after another, from united effects of want and contagious disease. We fear that these evils will never be remedied by the present government."

"Interesting that he doesn't mention Lord John Russell by name," said Joseph. "But here's a back-handed compliment if I ever saw one," naming his predecessor.

> "Though heartily despising the political inconsistency of Sir Robert Peel, still it must be admitted that when in power he evidenced a much greater amount of practical judgement in meeting the exigencies of the times than has ever been displayed by the present imbecile and apathetic administration."

He then went on to describe what James Brown of Donaghmore and so many others had feared:

"It is not alone in the south and west of Ireland that the horrors of starvation are experienced. <u>In our own immediate neighbourhood</u> the pressure of want is now severely felt, and the number of unfortunate individuals, who state too truly, with hunger pictured in their care-worn faces, that they have "neither meat nor money," is at present alarming. Hundreds of poor labourers daily throng our streets."

There was complete silence when Joseph finished reading. The coldest winter in Ireland's history had descended on the whole country. In some parts it snowed for two months without stopping. As Polly looked out of the window that night, all she could see at first was blackness. Then away in the distance, beyond the comforting shape of the old barn, she caught a glimmer of light, a small star twinkling as though hesitant to show itself on such a dark night. And there was another and another lower down in the sky. Except that this one was too low to be a star: It was a rush-light, set in the window by a family that could afford no Christmas candle and no matches, but had lit a rush from their own fields and from their own fire, honouring the ancient custom of lighting the way for Mary and her baby, and her husband, Joseph. As her mother Jane had done just hours before, holding her own baby in one arm while she set the rush-light carefully in the window, with William beside her. And as Polly watched them words that she had heard just that morning formed in her mind so clearly that she could almost see them: *and the light shines on in the darkness, and the darkness cannot quench it.* As she climbed up the steep stairs to bed, she said firmly to herself, the darkness cannot snuff it out.

CHAPTER XII

The Snow, Winter 1846-47

The snow fell and fell and fell. In the early days of the winter it had seemed a blessing, covering over all the misery with a white blanket, covering the hovels thrown up against every spare wall in Omagh. Covering the old graveyard on the hill with its raw new graves and the mass grave that held men, women and children. As it continued, it overwhelmed with its whiteness, blotting out the life of trees and beasts, freezing the last life out of the bones of exhausted men who had worked on the road until they fell.

Occasionally a figure appeared at the front door of Bridgewater Farm, seeking shelter from the storm. One night just as Jane was smooring the fire, turning the turf inward on itself, she saw a shadow passing the window. Even at this hour, someone was on the road seeking shelter.

When she opened the door, there was a young woman with three children clinging to her ragged skirt. The woman's pallor and the children's faces shocked her. They were the faces of little old people. She had seen many of these children when she was helping out at the postmaster's soup kettle in Dromore and up at the Grange, home of Lucas St. George. These waifs were beyond all she had seen.

"We're on our way to the poor house at Lowtherstown," the woman gasped. "They told us the way in the village, but it's farther than I thought. Would you have a corner of straw where we could lay our heads till the morning?"

Jane's heart sank, she had so little to offer. Then she remembered almost word for word the letter that an outraged citizen had sent to the *Impartial Reporter* about the conditions in the Lowtherstown Workhouse. There was no way she could send this woman and her children to that hell hole. She well recalled James Dill scolding her for exhausting herself caring for the sick and starving. But now, she also recalled her mother saying, "Look after those who have a call on you." She repeated this out loud half to herself. Eliza and Polly had already gone to find straw.

"If anyone has a call on us, this woman does," Eliza said defiantly as she produced a small horde of food from somewhere in a deep pocket in her skirt. More than once Jane had suspected her eldest of hiding portions of her own food to give out later. Just then, William came wearily in, carrying a pail of warm milk. Jane heated the milk and poured it over chunks of bread.

In the morning, Jane sent the family off with the last blanket her mother had made for her. She wondered if any of those children would still be alive in a week's time.

The Belfast News-Letter of Tuesday, February 7, 1847 reported Bread Riots in Monaghan. It went on to say in an editorial:

> *It is a period of the most acute anxiety to every reflective heart .... The accounts from the remote districts are becoming more and more intensely horrifying. We spare our readers the dreadful recital. Suffice it to say that throughout the whole western and south-western coasts of Ireland, the ascertained deaths by starvation are becoming too numerous for accurate record; they may be numbered by fifties and sixties in the day and many of the accounts are accompanied by details which cannot be penned nor read without the natural disgust which accompanies the recital of the most loathsome scenes.*

On February 5, the following Friday, the *News-Letter* stated simply: *We are verily, on the eve of the greatest crisis which has ever been experienced by the present generation.*

People were dying in every part of the country. The funds of the different relief committees were being exhausted.

In Dromore, Henry Lucas St. George did not know that when he sat down in his rectory on the evening of March 16, 1847 to write a desperate letter to the Tyrone Relief Committee.

> *I address you not knowing any other person to apply to ... I beg assistance in relieving the many poor creatures whom I meet every day. Since November nothing has been given to the poor except public works employing those able to work. Those without homes still beg from door to door. Many died from want. On Saturday last a woman lay down in an old shed of mine and was found late on Sunday evening almost dead. Many children have died as their parents have no food to give them.*

Local people had made an effort. The postmaster had set up a soup kitchen on Dromore's main street. Farmers continued to give what food they could to beggars at the door, but it was not enough.

St. George continued: *I did what I could, I have for the last five weeks every day — even Sunday, had meat soup with oatmeal and sometimes bread with it. Money was sent to me and with it I bought three barrels of oatmeal and some odd stores which I sold at half price ... Though I go on with the soup I cannot go on much longer.*

St. George was one of the landlords who no longer asked for rent from his tenants. The old and hated tithe system had been abolished. Now he wrote: *People crowd my house in hundreds daily and I can do little for them. If you cannot assist me,* he continued, *could you send this letter to someone who will?*

One young man who had been assisting at the Rector's soup kitchen during those terrible weeks was young Matthew Fleming, Polly's cousin and tormentor. Each time he came by the farm she noticed that he had grown quieter. She had seen him talking to the huge man brought up from Monaghan to bury the dead in the open graves, brought in from outside because local men no longer had the heart or the strength for it.

For some days during the bitterest part of that winter, Matthew had disappeared. When he returned he drew Polly aside. "It's been a heartbreaking time, Polly, as you know all too well. Some of the scenes have been too dreadful to talk about. I can't begin to imagine how people have been able to bear it, and it's far worse in other parts of the country. Something happened this last week, however, that I scarcely dare tell any one. I'm not sure they'd believe me."

"On the Tuesday, one of the parishioners came up to the Rectory to see if we could spare a little food. This young lad had an aunt living away up in the hills. He had been taking her food but had fallen ill on the heavy works program. I told Lucas St. George I would go with him. My horse is strong and could help break a trail through the snow. The young man looked exhausted, and I was as concerned about him as about his errand. To cut the story short we arrived after some difficulty at the aunt's cabin. There was no smoke coming from the roof, no footprints, no sign of life. When we went in, we saw the woman. It was clear we had brought food too late. She was barely alive, every bone on her showing through the skin. I sat down beside her and she reached out her hand. It was as though I was holding all the starvation in the world as I held her. She said to me in a whisper, 'This must be very hard for you.' In amazement at her thought for me I said, 'No, because there is such peace surrounding you.' And indeed there was, so palpable in that tiny hovel that I could almost feel it.

"Her nephew knelt beside her, and she said 'Come closer. There is something I want you to hear, and it is important, I feel,' and she emphasized every word. 'I feel a spirit of joy and laughter being given. And it has been absent for a long while.' We were both stunned, and then her nephew told her a funny story he had heard, and I came up with something too, and we sat there laughing, like the fools we were, in the midst of it all. It was quite clear to me then, (who would earlier have scoffed at such a thing), that this spirit was coming from Somewhere Else. I won't put more words to it than that.

It's not a story you'll read in any newspaper. Sometimes I wonder if I dreamed it all, but I'm sure not." Polly was sure too, though she looked hard at this cousin who had been her arch enemy. She would remember his story at the darkest moment in her life.

CHAPTER XIII

Lowtherstown Workhouse, 1847

In the past, Polly had often gone with her parents to the market day at nearby Lowtherstown.[8] Sometimes they walked, sometimes they took some of their pigs or cattle for sale. Sometimes they went by trap just for the fun of the outing. Jane had loved an excuse to look in the shop windows. Occasionally, she had bought a lovely bonnet to go with her scarlet cloak. William ran into many of his friends, local men like Hugh Maguire, descendant of the original aristocracy of the area.

Polly herself had loved the market with all its comings and goings, the tiny pigs who would escape from their owner and tumble over each other, squealing and tripping unwary passers-by. She would explore on her own, agreeing on a rendez-vous with Jane for lunch.

One day she had found herself on the Reihill Road leading past the newly built Lowtherstown workhouse. Someone had planted a lovely row of beech trees behind the sombre shadows of the workhouse building. Polly loved the way the beech leaves danced and rustled in

[8] *Now Irvinestown*

135

the sunlight. How could she know that there were children looking out of the workhouse windows at those same trees, children who had gone to bed with no supper that night and none the night before. By the summer of 1847, the Medical Inspector, Dr. Phelan, would describe conditions he found here as the worst in Ulster.

In early April, William had come back from the village with a copy of *The Impartial Reporter*. He was far from his usual debonair self. He began reading out loud a letter from someone who signed himself 'Humanitas' that started off, *Sir, I beg to call the attention of every humane man in the community to the way in which paupers are interred at our union workhouse — the graves not being more than eighteen inches deep, and in some instances the lids of the coffins are level with the ground. Is it any wonder that dogs should mangle the remains ...*

"William, in the name of God have you no sense? You'll be giving the child nightmares," broke in Jane, as she caught sight of Polly coming down the stairs. But Polly had heard and her mother was right. The story did indeed appear in her nightmares for years after, locked away so deeply that Polly, like many others, could never talk about it. It would be more than one hundred years before this story and countless others like it would be painstakingly excavated out of the stunned silence that surrounded them.

Polly heard her parents anguishing over the poor people who still turned up at their door. She watched her mother grow quieter and quieter. One day in February 1847, Jane called her children together. Somberly she told them, "Children, we've come to a decision. We are going to make a new life for ourselves, and it means we are going on a long journey, into an unknown place called Canada."

Polly was shaken to the core. How could she possibly leave Joseph and all her cousins, and uncles and aunts, and their dog Muff. She thought of her school friends one by one. The very thought of never seeing any of them again was more than a small ten-year-old could bear. And Bridgewater Farm itself, every inch of it rooted into her very being. Would she never again hear the laughter of the little brook with its stepping stones, or listen to rabbits and mice playing in the cornfields?

Polly knew from Joseph that Andrew, his younger brother the miller, would eventually take over the farm, and that at least was something. Polly knew well enough that countless other Irish families weren't as fortunate; too many of them had seen their homes torn down in front of their eyes, found themselves with no roof to shelter them, no family to care about them.

That winter Muff surprised them all by producing twins, having until that time shown no apparent interest in motherhood. Early in March, as the weather turned warmer, Polly dressed Isabella and Rebecca warmly and put them out in the yard to play with the puppies. Her mother was busy in the house washing and salting the new butter while William was cleaning out the cow stall in the byre. All of a sudden, Polly heard the sound of angry bleating in the lower field.

Running as fast as she could, she arrived at the edge of the field. There was Philomena, the sheep, frantically trying to fend off a pack of three snarling dogs, of the kind that had lately fed off carrion and dead bodies, while her one lamb huddled, terrified, under her flank. Polly shouted and waved her arms, but the dogs refused to back off. Then Cú Chulainn came to her aid, as eyes flashing and rolling back in their sockets, arms flailing, she rushed at the nearest dog, who took one look and fled.

Meantime a streak of fur had entered the fray. Muff snapped and snarled at the heels of the second dog who attempted to fight back but then thought better of it. The third dog was routed by young Joseph who had pelted down the hill after Polly, brandishing a stick. With a sigh of relief, Polly coaxed Philomena and her lamb back into the barn, and then turned to look for the twins. They were nowhere to be seen. Panic rising in her stomach, Polly called. No answer. She searched everywhere, followed by Muff who suddenly stopped beside one of the large willow turf creels that Joseph had been mending. Muff whined as she pawed the side of it. Polly lifted the creel, and sure enough, there were the twins, curled up in a ball fast asleep, a puppy clutched in each right arm. Polly heaved a sigh of relief and left Muff on guard while she and Joseph went to explore the possibilities of lunch.

CHAPTER XIV

William's Night in Omagh, early April 1847

In spite of worsening conditions, the *Tyrone Con* reported that the Omagh Fair was booming. Prices for horses were at an all-time high. Reluctantly, after a long debate with himself, William decided to sell his best horse to provide the fare for the family to Canada, with a bit over until he could find work.

On the first Saturday in April, William rode his horse, Ahasuerus, for the last time. Ahead of him were two of their best milk cows that would no longer be needed on the farm. The open space near the Omagh Courthouse was filled with squealing pigs. Dozens of homeless men wandered the streets looking for work. At the cloth market opposite the White Hart Inn, families were selling every stitch of clothing they could spare in order to buy food. The potato market in Brook Street was empty, but William headed for Cow Commons off Kevlin Road. After some hard bargaining, hand spitting and hand shaking, the cows were sold and he had coins in his pocket for the first time in months.

There was no turning back. In a sombre mood, he rode slowly toward the horse fair at the Dublin end of town. All too soon Ahasuerus was now the property of a florid man with a too-hearty laugh and a large purse. William disliked him at first sight, but he had little choice. The price the man offered was higher than he had dared to hope. Regretfully, William turned back along John Street, now filled with farmers and reeking with the usual evening fair day smell comprised of manure, and the odour of whisky and stout from the public houses along the way.

With the money jingling in his pocket, William could feel his old exuberance returning. He should be getting to the shipping agent before closing, but there was time. Earlier in the week, the man had told him there was a ship sailing from Derry for Quebec at the end of the month. The *Exmouth* was a fine copper-fastened whaler which had braved the Arctic ice; some people from Omagh had already booked. He'd better hurry.

Just then an old friend he used to race with grabbed his arm. The grandest card game was in full swing at the Abercorn Arms. Wouldn't he join them? Stakes were not too high! William had promised Jane never to gamble again. He hesitated; this was his lucky day, he thought. After all, he had once won his horse, Ahasuerus, at just such a game. He could add to his money for Canada; to refuse would be rude. Besides, he could always leave when he wanted.

To his annoyance, he found the same florid man who had bought his horse already seated at the table with several other men, one or two of whom he knew, all of whom welcomed him warmly. Too late to pull out. The time passed pleasantly enough. Drinks were served,

and his cards were half decent; the stakes were not too high; he had
won a few pounds.

Before he realized it, the stakes had risen, the florid man and his companion setting the pace. This is it, thought William, now in a reckless mood; either he would win tonight, or he and his family would stay in Ireland, as he wished they could in the very depths of his being. The cards would decide.

There was total silence around the table when William made his final bid. Appalled, his friends watched the florid man lay down his hand in what seemed like slow motion, then scoop up his winnings with a sneer and vanish out the door. No one had guessed it would come to this. They ordered another round of drinks, and then, one by one, rose and left their companion, sitting with his head in his hands.

"Too bad, but it's all the luck of the game," his friends murmured sympathetically, "Give him another drink," one or two of them told the bartender as they slapped down some coins and quietly drifted away.

The bartender was sweeping up the mess of cards and spilled liquor when he noticed one of the cards dropped carelessly by the stranger. "This is a marked card. You were had by a sharp one, my boy." William snatched the card from him and ran into the street.

A ragged child tugged at his sleeve, a little girl just the size of his daughter Maggie, so thin he could see the bones of her arms and legs. She had the shrunken look of an old woman who had lost everything. From an open doorway behind her came a reddish glow magnified by the fog. The dreadful moaning of someone in the final death throes of typhus, accompanied by the wail of a woman sounded from the house. It was a scene from Dante's *Inferno,* as gaunt figures swirled toward him through the falling snow. He stumbled over a bag of rags in a doorway, a person, whether dead or alive, he couldn't tell.

He wandered further, and heard cackling, swearing and mad raging that could only come from the Asylum of the Insane. Had he strayed that far? Soon he heard the rushing of water, and found himself leaning over a bridge, with the swirling water far below. For a moment he thought of throwing himself down, as many another had done. He retched violently, still clinging to the rail. He thought of his little son, Joseph, waiting trustingly for him at home; Jane, the baby, the wee twins, curled up asleep with Polly and Eliza.

And Joseph, his father. He had betrayed the trust of all of them. He could not return home. Even the prodigal son had stayed away for years. Sadly, William turned away from the river and back toward High Street. The stable-yard of the Abercorn Arms was still ablaze with light. In a far corner he found an empty stall, and some straw and there, finally, he lay down exhausted and fell into a deep sleep.

When William did not return home that night, Jane became nearly ill with worry. Had he been waylaid? Robberies were not unknown in these hard times.

The next morning a young lad arrived at the farm. He had a note for Jane. She read it and her anxiety turned to fury. Swiftly she wrote a return note saying that William might join them in Canada when it pleased him. Then she moved rapidly around the house, gathering up every object of value she could spare, including her wedding gifts, harnessed up the donkey, loaded the cart and drove off as fast as the little animal could go. She headed for the house of a man everyone called "auld skinflint" who was known as a moneylender and gombeen man. The obnoxious creature took one look at what she had brought, and then drawled slowly, "I'll give you enough for the passage for you and the children and a bit over if you'll throw in that red cloak of yours."

Jane gasped. The cloak had been made by her grandmother for her mother on her wedding day. Without a word, Jane unclasped the cloak and handed it over to the greedy creature. "Black is the latest fashion, so the *Con* says," she snapped as she strode out the door with the money safely in hand.

Joseph had never felt so profoundly powerless in his life. He knew that Jane was too proud to ask for help, and that his son was now on his own. There was nothing more he could do. As he prayed, he remembered something his own grandfather had said years before, during a terrible time when men were killing each other, "In the end, regardless of our choices, all that remains is the infinite mercy of God." That single sentence had stayed with him through some of the most difficult times in his life. Now it was all he had. It was enough.

Word of William's fall from grace had gotten around, thanks to Mrs. McAlistair's active tongue. Over the next two days, neighbours began arriving to commiserate. Jane accepted Hugh Maguire's offer of a horse and cart as far as Strabane. There was no one she would rather trust than this kindly man who knew everyone in the valley. They were to leave the first week in May.

The day before Jane was to go to Omagh to buy the tickets, a second note arrived. Polly recognized the handwriting. It was from her papa, William. She saw her mother's frown as she slowly opened the note. Jane gasped with surprise as she read, her cheeks flooding with colour. Polly hadn't seen her mother look so happy in days. Maddeningly, her mother wouldn't tell her what was in the note, except to say that the children would soon see their father and he had a surprise.

Late that night after Jane and the children were asleep, a tall figure appeared in the doorway. Joseph was asleep in his chair near the fire which was already banked for the night. He awoke with a start to see his son standing before him. The two talked long into that night. Before dawn William gave his father one last embrace and hurried away for the last time down the lane. When Jane came into the kitchen to make breakfast, she found Joseph still asleep where she had left him the night before.

For a long time, William told no one about his night in Omagh and the events of the next morning.

He had been awakened by the sound of voices shouting and the high whinny of a terrified horse. Outside on the street a crowd had gathered at a safe distance from the high-kicking heels of a thoroughbred trying to throw an equally terrified but determined young woman off his back.

In a few strides, William was at the head of the horse where a young stable-lad was hanging on to the bridle, at risk of being dragged along the rough cobblestones or trampled by sharp hooves, swearing at the top of his voice all the while.

Keeping his voice low, William soon had the animal steadied down. With a firm hand on the bridle he led horse and rider in through the arch to the stableyard of the inn.

"You can tell the lads, ma'am, if I may be so bold, not to give a horse like this a feed of oats first thing in the morning. It makes them too frisky and hard to handle."

"I've tried to tell them. It was terrifying coming down that steep hill by the courthouse, and then this creature darts right in front of us, a black cat of all things," the young woman replied, still out of breath and trying to regain her composure. Impulsively she reached into the purse hanging at her side and was about to offer William some coins.

Firmly he shook his head and turned away. The encounter with the horse had done more for him than he could possibly have done for himself at that moment, had given him confidence that he could be of some use in the world after all.

Later he learned from the innkeeper, John Harkin, who had witnessed the whole scene, that the young lady in question was one of the Hamilton family from the nearby estate of Baronscourt. "I've sent more than one of our lads up there this year; her uncle has found work for six hundred men on his place, unlike some of the landlords I could mention," he said, as he brought out an old

February issue of the *Tyrone Constitution*. A small paragraph was marked in red ink. It read *The hon. the Marquis of Abercorn is at present entertaining at Baronscourt. All are increasingly employed administering to the wants of the poor. During the last storm there was a third soup boiler set at work at the farm yard, which supplied two hundred and fifty families daily, besides a contribution of money to alleviate distress in the distant parts of the parish of Ardstraw. What a blessing to this parish they have been this year.*

"You might do worse than try up there yourself, but on the other hand, I could use some help around here with the horses, if you had a mind."

William spent that day working in the stable for his supper, feeding, grooming and bedding down the coach horses that came pounding in from Dublin and the north. Two nights later, John Harkin had news for him; the same florid man who had cheated him at cards was trying his tricks again, bold as brass, at another inn up the street. A little gentle persuasion might be in order.

No sooner did the man in question catch sight of William and the lads behind him than he picked up the cards in front of him, shoved back his chair, threw a purse full of coins right into William's face and fled out the back way. Stunned, William picked himself off the floor. There was his purse, with all the money he had lost and a few extra coins.

It was only years later that Jane heard the full story of William's night in Omagh, but neither she nor any of his children ever let him forget that he once had lost their fare to Canada.

CHAPTER XV

The Bog and the Fairy Thorn, May 1847

On the morning of that last day on the farm, Polly woke very early, unable to sleep. Dressing quietly, she climbed down the steep stairs from the loft, picked up a piece of bread from the fresh loaf her mother had baked the night before, and slipped out the front door. No one was about except one of the hens which cackled hopefully in search of a handout.

It was one of those lovely May days, a slight mist rising, and the early light glistening on cobwebs wet with dew. As she ran down the slope of the far field, Polly saw one of the cows lying peacefully among the rushes waiting for milking time, her calf dozing in front of her. A fine pale-gold ribbon of light edged the curved back of each of them. As if they were posing for their portraits, she thought, if only I could paint.

Restless, she ran on down through the tall grasses, oblivious of the odd nettle clinging to her skirt. There in front of her was the old willow tree, leaning over the rushing water of the Laughing Brook. She rested for a while, stretched out on the reassuring bulk of its rough trunk, listening to the ripple of the water as it eddied around the rocks beneath her.

Anxiously she listened for other sounds, the familiar rustling, scurrying, and squeaking of small creatures in the undergrowth, and the early-morning birdsong. The silence was eerie. People were saying that all the small field animals and even the birds were gone, gone to feed starving people.

Just then she heard a small sound near her, just a little way up the bank. It was Muff, who had quietly followed along behind her, stopped for a drink of water from the cool stream, and was now lying with her head on her paws, as if sharing in her unspoken loss. All around them the fields were full of the familiar small daisies and buttercups, mingled with the pale lilac of the cuckoo flower, the splashes of colour appearing and disappearing as the wind rippled through the long grass. Overhead white clouds drifted in a sunlit sky.

"Come on, Muff, we're going to the bog," Polly said with sudden determination, and off the two of them ran, Muff bounding and leaping to snap at flies. They didn't stay long, just the look and feel and smell of it for a brief moment was all Polly needed and all she could bear, holding in her mind's eye the picture of her grandfather throwing down the heavy turf to her father. Suddenly Polly became aware that she could think of him that way now without hindrance. No longer second-best as stepfather, with all the hesitations and difficulties that word implied, but as a father given to her by life at this moment when she badly needed one, who had given her little brothers and sisters she otherwise would never have known. And who helped them all stay alive at this moment.

It was as though something in her inner landscape had shifted once again. She left the bog at peace, the delicate white-flowered heads of the bog-cotton nodding companionably as she passed. Child and dog climbed their way out of the bog, over the rickety bridge and up the long slope towards home.

On the way they stopped for a moment in a mossy clearing among the rushes. To Polly's amazement, a small bundle of white fur was crouched on the far side of the clearing, almost hidden from sight. Another bundle appeared beside it and started to creep along looking for something to eat. Muff was just about to give chase, when young Joseph come bounding down the hill shouting "Polly, Polly, where are you?" When he saw her, he said accusingly, "We were all worried to death, where on earth have you been?" Polly shushed him, and beckoned him to watch the rabbits. A whole family of

them was now visible, pink noses twitching. And suddenly Polly knew with complete certainty that one day all the small animals and songbirds would come back, and some day in the future people would find all the food they needed from the earth.

"Let's go and say good-bye to our Fairy Thorn Tree," Eliza said to Polly late in the afternoon of their last day at Bridgewater Farm. Wasting no time, they hurried up the coach road and clambered carefully through the gap of the old stone fence, now broken down, with no one to mend it.

As they came closer to the Thorn Tree, alone in all its splendour in the middle of the field, the rose-gold light of the setting sun caught the branches. The two girls stopped, just close enough to the tree to let it know they were there, but not so close as to be disrespectful or offend its fairy guardians.

"Oh, Polly, however can I bear to leave this place?" cried Eliza. "It is so beautiful I think I might just die on the spot of a broken heart, like those Scottish princesses in olden times who died of grief, turning their faces to the ground," she added dramatically.

"You'll do no such thing," replied Polly firmly, repeating Eliza's own words back to her. "Don't you dare even think such a thing. If you died on the spot, who would tell the story? It would be a dreadful waste."

"Sometimes I wonder if anyone will ever know my story," sighed Eliza. "If I die, will you cross your heart and promise here beneath the Thorn Tree that you will tell my story, our story?" she added generously, seeing the look of dismay on her sister's face.

"I'll do no such thing, because you aren't going to die. I won't let you." Polly glared at her sister.

Eliza recognized that look and changed the subject. "We must remember this place for ever and ever, Polly, every detail of it. The way the drumlin hills roll in around us as though a giant hand had heaved them up and pushed and patted them into interesting shapes, with little valleys where sheep can hide and a horse or two. Here you never feel lonely, do you? Because the fields all around you are full of blackbirds and rabbits and badgers and hedgehogs and small mice squeaking and you can always hear calves or lambs calling in the distance."

Eliza stopped, her eyes clouding. "Or at least you could hear them until this last while. Now it is so silent in the fields around us. If I stop to think of all the neighbours who are gone, and all the awful things that have happened to people we know, I can hardly bear to go on."

In that moment Polly saw her sister's fragility, standing there with the golden light of the setting sun behind her. Already this person she thought she knew so well, with whom she had shared so many escapades and stories, seemed to be slipping away from her. Eliza was her closest friend, the one person she could talk to about their father, the house where they were born; and now she was losing her, this child-woman suddenly grown older than her years.

Polly shuddered as though a cold wind had come up. It was all she could do to keep the tears back. It was all too much, leaving home, leaving Joseph and the rest of the family and all her closest school friends. As she stood there, lost in sadness, the last light of the evening sun flared up, catching every shrub and stone in its light, silhouetting their Thorn Tree in all its elegance and lighting up the edges of the clouds in a way that took her breath away.

The sisters said good-bye to the Thorn Tree and climbed back over the old stone fence, hurrying now, knowing their mother would be anxious. Away off to their left a cluster of rain clouds were piling up, casting dark shadows over the fields as they passed overhead.

"I do wish I could see just one more rainbow before we leave. Or is that too much to ask for?" said Polly.

"It's much too late in the day, more's the pity," sighed Eliza, as they turned the corner onto the coach road.

Polly was just stubborn enough to keep looking anyway. You never know, she thought, shivering a little as the storm clouds came nearer and a few drops of rain began to fall. She couldn't believe her eyes. There in the middle of the dark cloud bank was a little glimmer of a rainbow, a tiny fragment of colour, appearing and almost about to vanish.

"Look, Eliza, look," she cried. "There it is, just when we thought it wasn't possible. The littlest rainbow you ever saw in your life, come especially to say good-bye to us."

"That's your rainbow, Polly, and you are to remember it for ever and ever." Eliza hugged her sister, and the two of them raced for the doorway of home as the rain came pelting down.

CHAPTER XVI

The Road to Drumquin, May 9, 1847

Later in life Polly would remember only fragments of that slow trip by cart away from Dromore towards an unknown future.

Her last glimpse of her grandfather, Joseph, came after the goodbyes were all said, as he stood in the doorway of the old house, Muff at his side, waving good-bye until they were out of sight. She would never forget the look on his face.

"Here we have no abiding place," he had said to her quietly, so quietly she had almost not heard. That night he wrote all of their names in the family Bible, the date, May 9th, 1847, and three words *"Today they left."*

Polly would remember some of the neighbours walking with them part of the way, Eliza laughing as they rumbled through the tiny shimmering grove of birch trees on the outskirts of Dromore, one of her favourite places; a boy from her class at school walking with them until nightfall, only then saying a wistful good-bye.

The road running high along the broad slope of the mountain, avoiding the deeper gorge below. Bessy Bell and Mary Grey in the distance, the two mountains whose names had given rise to many a story and then the church tower of Omagh, in its jewel-like setting, glistening in the sun.

They passed a stone cottage and the family came out with part of a loaf of fresh bread and some milk for the children, rarities in those hungry days, then walked with them as the road took a sharp left-hand turn up a steep hill. The sun-drenched branches of golden whin and whitethorn met almost overhead there. So powerful was the perfume of their flowers after the rain that it stayed with them for miles, it seemed.

There was a brief stop at McCanney's pub so Hugh Maguire could chat with some of his friends. Then on to Kirlish Castle, where the children played hide-and-seek, their laughter echoing away along the ruined walls, where curlews once flew.

While the children played, Jane discovered that their friend, Hugh Maguire, had been named after an ancestor, one of the most important chieftains in Ulster, who had led the cavalry in the Battle of the Yellow Ford. This was one of the biggest military defeats of the English army in Irish history, on the 14th of August 1598, during the Nine Years War. Jane hadn't been very interested in history, at least the way it was taught at her school, but standing here beside the ruins of Kirlish Castle and listening to Hugh's stories about the O'Neills and the O'Donnellys, made those old times seem much more vivid. Her own family was distantly related to the Caldwells of Castle Caldwell in Fermanagh, who had fought on the other side of that same war. And she could tell Hugh she had grown up on a farm in Fermanagh, near Lisnaskea, not far from the legendary Fairy Thorn where generations of Maguire chieftains had been sworn in. Often she had gone with her mother to visit the old Aghalurcher graveyard, where Phairs and Nobles and Flemings were buried side-by-side with Maguires.

On the next stretch of road they were almost forced into the ditch as the stagecoach for Londonderry thundered past. Jane was relieved that she and her family were not among the hurrying travellers. This slow elegiac ride through the May beauty of the countryside, with the steady creak-creak of the wheels and the clopping of the patient horses, seemed more in keeping with the depth of her own emotions. They passed other families who were walking, walking all the way to the port. She wondered if they would arrive safely.

That night they stayed with the Flemings in Drumquin. The children fell asleep almost immediately on the straw mattress on the floor. Sleep did not come easily to Jane. She sat up talking with William's cousins until the small hours of the morning. They had always been easy to talk to, and in earlier years had been frequent visitors to the house on Bridgewater Farm. Now they talked about the devastation in the Drumquin area. Jane had seen with her own eyes the blackened and empty lazy-beds along the sides of the mountain.

John Fleming, himself a farmer, spoke of his outrage at some of the landlords in his area who had insisted on their rents no matter what. If a farmer had three or four fields of corn, the landlord would say that one field would do him rightly, and the rest was loaded onto ships at Belfast, sometimes under armed guard. "They don't seem to realize they are trading on people's lives. I can't understand the mentality," he said.

"And all this while there are people going from our area to Capehill in Dromore Parish, where they get a handout of a long can of porridge, which won't last the week for a family with children. People are dying in hundreds and there is a man from Dromore Parish named Reilly, who has been employed to haul the corpses away on a barrow to be buried. We've heard that they take them to a field opposite Golan Mill. Some of the farmers have been kept alive by people like the Moffitts of Magherenny, more power to them, who have handed out porridge from a large boiler in their yard, as the Quakers have done in many other parts of the country."

The next morning, Jane bundled the sleepy-eyed children once more into the cart. The hours went by and she found herself scarcely able to stay awake.

And then suddenly they were in Strabane, and Polly, to her amazement, caught sight of a tall familiar figure. Joseph, Robert, Maggie and the twins tumbled over each other in their excitement at seeing their father, William. Before they knew it, he had whisked them in the direction of a small train that stood puffing and snorting at Strabane Station. "We're going to ride on a twain," lisped Robert, nearly beside himself with joy. Soon they were on board, chugging along on this first completed lap of the new Enniskillen-Londonderry line. The smoke from the little engine blew back into the open carriages where they sat huddled together, as the engineer shovelled coal for all he was worth, exposed equally to wind and weather. Never mind, they were on the move.

Halfway to Derry the train gave a little cough and a lurch as it struggled up an incline, belched an extra puff of smoke then ground to a halt. Immediately all the passengers climbed down from their seats and gave the engine an encouraging push. With an indignant puff and a final belch, it started up again and everyone scrambled aboard. A moment of joy that Polly would remember long after.

As the little train chugged into the Gallows Strand terminus on the far side of the River Foyle, William pulled out the tickets from his pocket. They were going to sail on the *Sesostris*, he announced. It was due to sail sometime in the next three days, as soon as the wind made up its mind to blow in the right direction. They might have to spend a night or two in Londonderry, and so it turned out. Lodging was scarce, with so many people waiting and hoping for passage, but they found a room on the third floor at the back of a rooming house. The narrow staircase leading up to it smelled of stale cabbage and other unpleasant odours, but it was a roof over their heads.

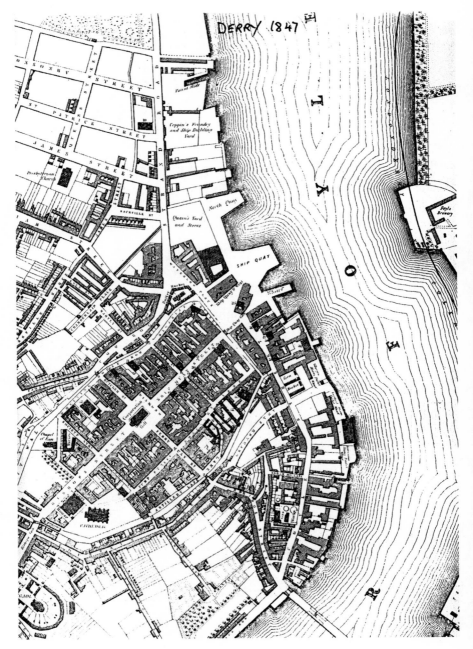

J & J Cooke, Office, yard and quay, Londonderry / Derry, 1847.

CHAPTER XVII

Londonderry, May 1847

Polly and the children had never seen such a city as Derry. They spent hours clambering over the high stone walls that held so much history of siege and saint, of oak groves and daring young apprentice boys. Even at night most of the streets were bright with the new gaslights. By day, Ships Quay was a thronging mass of shouting sailors, baggage handlers, ticket sellers, fish mongers, and hucksters, all clamoring for the attention of passengers desperate to find passage. It was an exciting place to be if you were young and held a ticket on one of the sailing ships floating at anchor in the safest harbour in Ireland.

The *Sesostris* was one of these. A magnificent three-masted vessel built on the coast of Scotland, chartered by J. & J. Cooke, with an experienced captain, Mr. Dand, in charge. William could hardly contain his excitement. At last, his dream of sailing in a real ship towards who knew what adventures had come true.

And perhaps one day he would own his own farm. The youngest children, Robert, little Maggie and the bouncy two-year-old twins Isabella and Rebecca all caught his excitement. Young Joseph spent the whole day exploring the port with his father.

Polly and her mother soon retreated back to the shops of the upper town, looking wistfully at provisions they could neither afford nor take on board. Others were worse off; some families had long ago given up hope of a passage anywhere. Famine had hit hard and early in this most northern part of Ireland. The population of the Inishowen Peninsula had been devastated, the workhouse in Derry overwhelmed by the number of applicants.

That night, Polly returned reluctantly to their dismal lodging that was so unbearably different from the farm they had left. She felt as though her inmost spirit was cramped up by the narrow walls, the smells, and the suffering she had seen in the eyes of children all day long.

She stood for a long time at the window of the tenement house looking out over the roof tops with the sun setting slowly in the far western horizon. Then, to her amazement, she heard a familiar song, faint at first, then growing stronger, vibrant in the clear air. There was a solitary blackbird perched jauntily on the nearby soot-blackened rooftop, singing his heart out with his special evening song, almost as though he had deliberately chosen her for an audience. For nearly an hour she listened entranced, beckoning her mother and Eliza to join her. Through all that followed, she would never forget the blackbird's song.

The next morning, she and the younger children stumbled sleepily down the steep stairs. They found their mother, wee Jane and Eliza already seated in the kitchen staring at small bowls of something that was supposed to be porridge. "More like frog spawn," Joseph pronounced, setting down his spoon after one mouthful.

Jane was listlessly looking over a week-old newspaper half-covered with stains. It was a copy of the **Northern Whig**, dated May 4, 1847. Their landlady had handed it to her with a smirk, pointing to a headline that read:

DREADFUL SHIPWRECK ON THE COAST OF ISLAY – TWO HUNDRED AND FORTY LIVES LOST

*We received this morning, through the kind attention of Captain Stewart, of the **Thetis**, a copy of the **Glasgow Herald**, of yesterday morning, containing a circumstantial account of the loss of the **Exmouth**, which left Londonderry on Sunday, April 25th, bound for Quebec, with emigrants. The news reached Glasgow, on Saturday, as stated in our shipping intelligence, by three seamen, by the **Modern Athens** steamer, being the only survivors of the wreck. The description given of the disaster is most afflicting. They say the ship was ground and crunched so dreadfully, that she must have gone to pieces immediately. There were three ladies on board, cabin passengers. The great mass of the emigrants must have perished in their berths, as the rocks rapidly thumped the bottom out of the vessel. Up to Thursday evening, twenty bodies had been washed ashore at Islay, but the total number lost cannot be calculated at fewer that two hundred and forty souls.*

John Cooke;
Owner of the Sesostris.

Ad for one of John Cooke's ships,
Doctor Kane, *sailing from*
Derry (Londonderry) to Quebec,
Canada; 23rd June, 1864.

The Departure; Engraving from Illustrated London News; *July 6, 1850.*

Furious and upset, Jane thrust the newspaper back into the hands of their landlady, snatched up her baby, beckoned Eliza and Polly to follow her with the younger ones, and marched out the front door of the rooming house.

Polly and Eliza exchanged worried looks as they hurried after their mother down Ship Quay Street, under the arched gate and into the harbour area. Almost directly in front of them were some of the McCorkell ships, an impressive sight as they lay at anchor, moored to the quay. Veering to the left, Jane threaded her way through a crowd of vendors, seamen, dockworkers and onlookers until she came to the warehouse of J. & J. Cooke. She had been told that the senior partner, John Cooke, lived right on the premises; he was sure to be close at hand. She saw a rather distinguished looking man with bushy sideburns and eyebrows, a long nose and generous mouth, standing near the entrance of the warehouse, intent on studying a sheaf of papers held firmly in his left hand. None other than the man she was looking for, she learned from a lad heaving barrels.

"What guarantee can you give me, Sir, that we are not about to suffer the same fate as the *Exmouth*?" she demanded of the startled man, bypassing the usual courtesies.

"Madam, I am not in the habit of drowning passengers," John Cooke replied with some asperity, annoyed at the interruption. Then seeing the look on the face of the woman before him, holding her baby, his tone softened, "I assure you, Ma'am, that J. & J. Cooke is noted for its safety record. We and the McCorkells have transported thousands of passengers across the Atlantic without mishap. We don't run 'coffin ships' if that's what is worrying you." When he learned the Flemings were travelling on the *Sesostris*, he informed her that Captain Dand was one of the most experienced men in the business. He would not make the same error as the unfortunate master of the *Exmouth* who, in the midst of a blinding tempest, had mistaken a lighthouse on the Scottish Isle of Islay for the Tory Island light. In fact, of the fifty or so sailing ships that left from the port of Derry that year, only the *Exmouth* was shipwrecked.

Reassured, Jane thanked him and went down to have a look at the *Sesostris* where it lay at anchor. There they found William and young Joseph who were absorbed in watching the sailors loading supplies. Jane had also been told by John Cooke that he agreed to Captain Dand's insistence that a properly trained ship's surgeon be part of the crew. James Burnie, a University of Edinburgh graduate, had been hired by the captain before the ship left Scotland under lease to J. & J. Cooke. Now James was overseeing the loading of barrels of water, and lime juice, and sufficient quantities of vinegar as a disinfectant.

With the crowds, the seagulls flying overhead, the salt smell of the sea tide in the river, the shouts of the sailors and the white sails rippling overhead, the children and their mother were loathe to leave the harbour. They were still waiting for the wind from home, as William described the wind coming from the direction of Dromore, to carry their ship on the morning tide up the river, through Lough Foyle and out of the protection of the natural harbour to the sea.

That night, as Jane was telling William all about the events of the day, she couldn't help laughing a little. "As I was standing there listening to Mr. Cooke talk about his ships with so much pride,

I couldn't help remembering my grandmother. She always kept a little hand-written sign by her bedside. It said in bold letters, 'Write failures in dust, blessings in granite.'" William wondered if she yet realised, as he had done, that if he had not lost their fares that night in Omagh, they would all have been passengers on the *Exmouth*.

Later they learned that among those who perished on that terrifying night in April, were some of Jane's Caldwell relatives; James, Margaret and Mary Caldwell, five children and one small infant; a woman from Omagh named Ann Alone; and John Wilson from Shaneragh with his family of three.

Emigrants, London Illustrated News; *1849*.

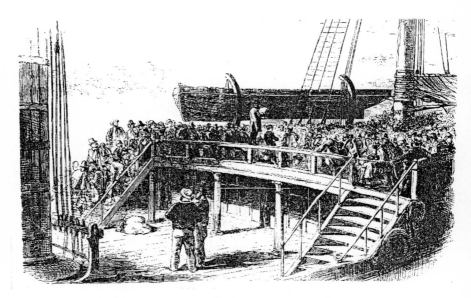

Quarter Deck of an Emigrant Ship – The Roll-Call;
Engraving from Illustrated London News; *July 6, 1850.*

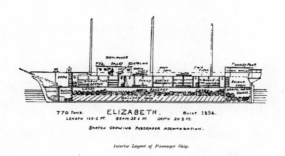

770 TONS.   ELIZABETH.   BUILT 1856.
LENGTH 140·6 FT.   BEAM 33·6 FT.   DEPTH 20·3 FT.
SKETCH SHOWING PASSENGER ACCOMODATION.

Interior Layout of Passenger Ship.

CHAPTER XVIII

The *Sesostris,* May 14, 1847

William climbed up to the crowded deck where he found James Burnie dividing the able-bodied passengers into crews for clean-up and pumping out the hold in rough weather. A fiddler was playing, and a few of the younger people were dancing in a small cleared space. Polly, Eliza and Joseph stood at the the railing watching the walls of Derry recede in the distance, as the current carried the ship up the river and into the broad expanse of Lough Foyle, one of the safest inland harbours in Ireland. The meadows along the slope of the hillside were dotted with sheep, which turned into tiny white toys with two legs shorter than the others, as the ship sped along.

A woman standing near them at the rail told them she was from Londonderry. "Now we're passing the wee village of Muff," she said, pointing to a cluster of small houses.

"So Muff even has a village named after her; she'll be famous one day," exclaimed Joseph proudly.

Polly decided to quickly think of something else so she wouldn't burst into tears. "There's Captain Dand," she exclaimed as she saw him climbing down into the tender, which would drop him at Culmore. He was taking back the Custom House Certificate completed by the agent. The official port records for posterity would show three hundred and six passengers on the *Sesostris*, much to the Captain's annoyance; he knew the rest were being smuggled on board at Moville, under cover of darkness, after the pilot had left them. Soon they passed the massive shape of Binevenagh on their starboard side and by nightfall were docked at Moville, where the extra passengers were quietly brought on board. 428 men, women, and children found their way into their cramped quarters. No one noticed a few canny rats that tightrope-walked their way up to the ship's hold.

The next morning, as they passed Greencastle and Magilligan Point, and rounded Inishowen Head, into the open sea, some of the passengers took to their bunks, overcome by the motion of the ship. Then Jane stayed up with William and the children as long as possible, grasping the railing for dear life. She wanted to hold the last sight of Ireland firmly in her mind. As they passed Malin Head, the Lloyds' Tower acknowledged their passing with a signal, which in turn would be transmitted to London for insurance purposes. Jane wondered if any of her family would ever come back. Somehow she was sure that she would not.

During those first few days, James Burnie had his hands full trying to persuade his passengers to heave themselves out of their bunks where they lay groaning, and get themselves up on deck where at least the air was fresh. Last thing at night he made a brief notation in his diary as his uncle had taught him:

Our course W.N.W. — then W.S.W. Steerage passengers
finally forming themselves into groups of three or four to cook
what little they can, mostly porridge and eggs while they last.
Gave lime juice to a woman who was quite ill.

Jane came to know some of the other mothers as they struggled
to keep their footing while stirring porridge over a fire set into a
brick-lined hearth on the deck. Margaret McCaffrey was from
Enniskillen and knew some of Jane's Caldwell and Noble relatives.
Jane Riddle was from Maguire's Bridge. She and her husband,
James, had children about the same age as her own. Elizabeth
Cunningham and her husband, Andrew, were from Omagh and
knew some of their friends there. Over the weeks at sea a bond was
formed between most of the passengers, although James Burnie had
to intervene when one of the men was caught stealing food at night.
A jury of his peers sentenced him to a week's duty cleaning out the
water closets, the only sanitation facility for the steerage deck. The
offence was not repeated.

James was beginning to congratulate himself on how well things
were going. This was his first major voyage since graduating from
Medical School. Then abruptly the tone of his diary changed. On
the sixth day out he noted:

Lat. 55 deg 50'00''. Heavy seas with rain and lightning. All
hands to the pumps. Deck so slippery with salt hard to keep
your footing. Passengers stayed below, unable to cook. Death
of two of the smallest babies, William Byers, aged one, and
Jane Fleming aged nine months.

Jane accepted the death of her baby with resignation. She had
known from the beginning that these long sea voyages took their toll

of small infants. She and the mother of William Byers comforted themselves with the routine of each day, the preparation of meals such as they were, the never-ending struggle to keep clothes and bedding in some degree of cleanliness. Eliza gathered some of the children together in a circle and told them a story she had heard from Arthur Slevin, the Dromore schoolmaster, about the Trojan horse, the beauty of Queen Helen, the Fall of Troy and the Golden Apple that had caused it all, stretching the last part a little while she handed out pieces of dried yellow apple that their friend Catherine Hamilton had brought them.

Eliza and Polly had first met Catherine when they ventured to the edge of the Lakemount Estate to see if any of the apples there might have fallen on the road, where they would be public property. As they searched, a shower of apples had fallen around them, and a merry face had appeared among the branches. From then on, Catherine became their friend. She was the daughter of the shoemaker on the estate, and had been married in one of the last weddings at the old church on the Brae. Before they left, she had brought a kerchief full of dried apple as a present for Eliza and Polly. One of the mothers told Jane later that she thought this gift shared by Eliza had perhaps saved the life of her own little girl, who until then had been listless and sickly.

On the twelfth day at sea, Wednesday May 26, Captain Dand saw through his binoculars an ominous bank of cloud forming in the distance, with the white crest of huge waves already visible. He gave orders to heave to, reef in all sails, secure every moveable piece of baggage, utensils or equipment, batten down the hatches, and make sure the pumps were fully working. The storm, the heaviest he had ever experienced, hit just before midnight.

James Burnie wrote nothing in his diary that night. It carried a brief entry the following night.

Sea rose in waves as high as the main mast, sending the vessel rolling in the most awful manner. Scarce any of the seamen could keep their footing on the deck. Kegs full of water for immediate use rolled in every direction, colliding with buckets full of unnameable filth. At the far end of steerage a section of bunks came loose from its fastening ... Here the diary broke off. James Burnie had not been able to bring himself to complete it.

James had gone down to steerage during a lull and had found ten-year-old Polly holding the body of her little brother in her arms. His skull had been crushed by the heavy weight of the bunk as it came crashing down. No one knew how little Robert had come to be there; Polly had thought he was safe with their parents. The fact remained, he was gone from them, not from typhus or starvation like so many other Irish children, but from one of life's random accidents.

In its very singularity and unexplainability this tragedy brought the people of the ship closer together. They had come from villages and townlands all over Northern Ireland; in the beginning some had been deeply isolated in their own grief, loss, and fear of an unknown future; their sense that even the land had deserted them. Perhaps that hard-hearted Trevelyan in Whitehall was right to think that God was punishing the Irish. Even a Trevelyan could not have explained the mystery of the death of this one small boy whom all who knew him loved and no one could accuse of failure in God's sight.

In the beginning Polly had felt just a little isolated surrounded by so many Catholics at close quarters, many of them speaking Irish, even though she was friends with Catholic children and had often been in their homes. Now she found the sound of the rosary, begun by one of the older women, comforting in its quieting rhythm, not unlike the sound of the waves, now heard lapping more gently against the ship's hull. Her own prayers were wordless, welling out of a grief deeper than tears. She felt rather than heard the kind words of strangers — "Sorry for your trouble" — saw the way the other women gathered around her mother, the men awkwardly present in the shadows behind them.

Jane took off her beautiful red scarf, and placed it gently over the small body, before the sailors lifted little Robert up the ladder to the upper deck. The Captain said a brief prayer. Later Polly could scarcely remember all that happened next. She knew only that Robert had disappeared into the sea, that her mother never wore red again and that they never spoke of that voyage.

For days Polly had blamed herself for the accident. Why had she not kept better watch over her small brother. Then one day an older woman said quietly to her, "Polly, you must never, never blame yourself for what happened. We aren't perfect; we're only human and we can't possibly foresee or forestall all that happens even to the people we love most. As well blame the sea, or the agent who overbooked, or the deckhand who missed a nail or two. This was neither your fault nor was it God's will, in this imperfect world.

Lay your heart to rest, and know that somewhere out there will be another child who needs your love, and you will love him or her twice as much because of your little brother."

The sailors continued their dangerous work of going aloft to either furl or unfurl the sails and then scramble up the rigging to the yards, edging out along the footropes with nothing holding them except the weight of their bodies hanging over the spar, at risk of falling backwards if the ship lurched.

The weather continued to be rough, as if determined to make life as miserable as possible for the passengers. Most remained confined to their deck, but the hardiest, William among them, took their turn at the endless pumping. And every morning the decks had to be swabbed to keep a safe footing. James Burnie continued his rounds, doling out lime juice to those most in need of it, the elderly and the sick.

On the third night of rough weather, little Maggie took ill, her whole body hot with fever. Jane held her in her arms, trying to pour her own strength into her child, but in her heart she felt her brother's death had been just one shock too many for the little girl. At about four o'clock in the morning, Maggie's life ebbed quietly away. Jane stayed where she was, unable to bear the sight of one more burial, as William carried the small body up the steep stairs for the last time.

Jane felt overcome by a tremendous lassitude, a seawall of grief loosening her hold on life. If after all the effort, all the struggle she was going to lose one after another of her family, why go on? They might just as well have stayed where they were and waited for the fever to take them as it had so many.

The entry in James Burnie's diary was very brief that night. It was only years later that he learned not to take the death of someone in his care, especially a child, as a failure on his part.

Over the next few days, the wind shifted yet again. The great sails were unfurled to their full capacity, allowing the ship to run fast at a good ten knots. The passengers were able to get back up on deck; some did a little washing. One of the men took out his fiddle and tried a familiar song from home. A pair of the more sure-footed young people tried out a step or two and soon a whole group were dancing, only to find themselves careening madly towards the railing when a sudden wave tilted the ship forward. William tried to persuade Jane to join them on deck, but she seemed unable to summon up the strength.

The next morning, as she lay in the bunk, she caught sight of a familiar small figure struggling up the steep ladder towards the open hatch. It was her daughter, Polly, one hand firmly clutching the family chamber pot, now full to the brim and in danger of spilling its odorous contents over the child's clothes, the other hand hanging on to the stair railing for dear life as the ship lurched in the trough of a wave.

A sense of the ridiculous swept over Jane and she began to laugh, her whole body shaking with waves of emotion, just shy of hysteria, releasing the pent up grief and despair, breaking through the paralyzing numbness. As Jane rose to her feet, she saw two arms reach down through the hatch and take the chamber pot from Polly. Her father, William, had arrived just in time. Jane beckoned to a couple of the other parents standing nearby and they formed a chain, passing the loaded buckets and chamber pots from hand to hand and up through the hatch. A tiny defiant gesture on the side of life and survival.

James Burnie came down to steerage at this point and encouraged every last person who could move to come up on deck. The straw-filled mattresses were lifted up, some of the contents thrown out and the bunks scrubbed down with vinegar. Fresh straw was brought where needed and the hatches left open to let fresh air circulate.

Up on deck, Jane rested her body against the railing as she watched seagulls circling around the white sails high overhead, feeling herself gently rocked by the motion of the ship running before the wind. Almost as if I were being re-parented, she thought in surprise, with William and Eliza beside her, Polly and the twins nearby.

Just then a large rat scurried across the deck, causing Eliza to shriek in fright. "They sneak up the ropes when we're in port if we don't keep a sharp lookout," said a rough voice behind them. The second mate had a large tawny-coloured cat perched on his shoulder, which promptly leapt onto the deck and took off after the rat. No rats allowed here, was the motto of this crew, who numbered about thirty.

Young Joseph was up ahead with one of the sailors who was showing him how to tie a knot and how to shimmy up a rope. He was six feet up one of the ropes when he gave a great whoop and pointed, nearly losing his grip in his excitement. There ahead of them was a spout of water shooting straight up, with a dark shape moving just below the surface of the water. It was their first sighting of a whale, and soon they could see a whole pod of the creatures. One of the whales leapt in the air then dived straight downward, the huge tail causing barely a ripple.

As they stood watching, it occurred to William to tell a story he had heard from his mother. Her maiden name was Molly Nelson. She had always understood that she was descended in some way from the hero of the Battle of Trafalgar in the Napoleonic Wars. The Admiral, Horatio Nelson, had stood on the bridge all through the fierce battle, with ships sinking all around him. At the very moment when victory was certain, he had been struck down by a cannonball. His body was brought home in triumph by his comrades, pickled in a barrel of brandy, while his mistress, Lady Hamilton, waited in vain for the return of her hero.

As Jane listened, it occurred to her that nearly every Irish person had some sort of heroic story in their background making everyday life more interesting.

"Did you ever regret that you didn't go to sea?" she asked for about the fifth time, sure of the answer.

"This one journey will last me the rest of my life," William answered grimly. "My aim now is to get all of us safely settled on a farm as soon as possible."

James Burnie noted their location: *latitude 44 deg. n., longitude 47 deg. w., 48' 15''*

The ship had by now reached the Sand Banks off the coast of Newfoundland, the water shallow enough to take a sounding. Schools of porpoises and dolphins appeared quite close to the ship. The sea no longer felt so vast and lonely to Polly, now that she knew all those creatures made their home in it.

About five miles in the distance, they could see land with dark cumulous clouds building over it. As dusk came on, everyone stayed up on deck, reluctant to lose sight of land. Flashes of lightning lit up the sky, forerunners of a storm. All of a sudden, William noticed a soft bluish light illuminating the great mast overhead, and running along the yard arm. A soft rain began to fall and every drop seemed infused with this bluish light. Jane, Eliza, Polly and the younger ones stood close beside him, watching in amazement as the ghostly flames danced around the masts, accompanied by a strange buzzing sound.

"It's St. Elmo's Fire," said one of the sailors. "I've heard about it all my life, but this is the first time I have ever seen it. It's a good omen. It means fair weather is ahead. You can even hold your hand in it and it won't hurt you. Our Captain told us even Shakespeare knew about this, with those lines in the Tempest *now on the beak, now in the midst, the deck, in every cabin I flamed amazement.*"

James Burnie stayed up late the next few nights, talking to the sailors, watching the stars come out. He marvelled as the ship at last entered the St. Lawrence. The river was two hundred miles wide at this point, so vast you could not see the far shore. On the second evening when they anchored close to shore to take on a pilot, and fresh eggs, milk, bread, and water, he watched the changing colours of the river, deep turquoise close to shore, mingling with the almost purple shadow of the mountains, whose heavily wooded slopes came down close to the water. James was from a naval family; the sea was in his blood. Still he would be glad when this particular journey was over. He sensed trouble ahead.

CHAPTER XIX

Grosse-Île
Monday, June 14, 1847

The same day as the *Sesostris* entered the St. Lawrence, June 10, another ship, the *Agnes* from Cork, dropped anchor two miles downstream from Grosse-Île. It could get no closer, even though the Captain and most of the crew were ill, twenty-nine of its passengers had died at sea, and thirty-five more would die as the ship waited to land. Ninety-six of the passengers who were carried off the ship later died in the hospital that had just been erected on the island.

On June 14, the day the *Sesostris* approached Grosse-Île, a hospital matron wrote down her impressions and sent them anonymously to the *Journal de Québec*. They were published three days later.

Journal de Québec June 17, 1847:

> *I arrived here with about two hundred and fifty tents on May 27th. Forty sailing ships were in quarantine, with perhaps ten*

thousand passengers aboard, hundreds of whom were sick. They could not be taken ashore, however, because of a lack of sheds. I set to work pitching tents for sick people whose condition seemed most promising. Even if I had wanted to provide shelter for those whose recovery looked doubtful, I would not have had room for one-tenth of them. It was impossible to enlist the help of enough women and domestics ... so when I had time, I worked as a matron in the hospitals, giving the sick something to drink and washing their sores.

I cannot describe the horrors and misery I saw ... at least thirteen hundred terrible cases of typhus, in addition to smallpox and measles. People died right before our eyes at all hours of the day. The bodies were taken to the dead house in wheelbarrows, thrown on wood chips and left there until nightfall. They were then placed in coffins that were piled onto carts and transported to the cemetery. People perished in much greater numbers on the vessels than in the hospitals.

SHIPS ARRIVING AT GROSSE-ÎLE

Name	Port of	Crossing Days	Steerage	No. of Deaths	No. of Deaths in Quarantine
Jessie	Limerick	56	479	56	26
Lady Hastings	Cork	34	454	72	48
Sesostris	Londonderry (Ireland)	31	428	12	8
William	Belfast	45	407	11	7
Total			1,768	151	89

By then, Alexander Buchanan from Omagh, Chief Emigration Agent, had chartered a second small steamship to take passengers off the ships onto the island. Finally it was the turn of the passengers of the *Sesostris*.

As soon as the whole boatload had been safely off-loaded onto dry land, the families were hurried to the eastern end of the island, as far away from the sick people as possible. There they found a rough village of the tents purchased by Alexander Buchanan, hastily put together, many of them already occupied.

By the time darkness came that night the whole family was settled down to sleep. As Polly drowsed off, exhausted, she could hear a small animal rustling in the grass nearby, a dog barking, and waves gently lapping against the nearest shore. "Robinson Crusoe would have loved this island," Eliza had whispered to her and the twins as their ship approached the dock at last.

I wonder, Polly thought to herself as she fell asleep.

The next morning after a scanty breakfast, the first order of the day was washing, washing, washing. All the new arrivals headed for a small inlet near the dock and what a scrambling and a splashing and a slapping of wet clothes on rocks there was. And a release of pent up laughter. You'd have thought a party was in progress. Jane returned to the tent with armloads of assorted wet garments that had long since lost their shape and colour, the scantily dressed children trailing behind her like a flock of small ducklings. Soon all the bushes around the tent village were covered with the wet clothing of four hundred people.

The next morning Polly took young Joseph and the twins off to explore a little cove nearby. Soon Joseph was running up and down the stretch of sand shouting at the seagulls that dipped and dived overhead. Polly closed her eyes for a moment as the twins played happily in the sand. When she came to with a start, Joseph was nowhere to be seen. Panicking, she began to search until suddenly a head appeared on the far side of a large outcropping of rock. Then the rest of him came into sight, dripping blue-grey mud from head to toe, looking like a slippery small seal. His face was a picture of dismay, so woeful Polly forgot to scold. Just then, Jane and William came into sight. Joseph ran towards them and ended up clutching his father's trouser legs, smearing it with blue mud in the process. To Polly's amazement, her mother ignored the mud that landed on her own newly-washed skirt and simply sank down on the nearest stretch of sand. For what seemed like an eternity, they sat together watching the swirling water of the river through the long hours, listening to its sound as the sea tide came and went, watching a great blue heron standing in motionless elegance, one foot tucked under a wing, as though it were waiting for something important to happen.

"Where's Eliza?" Polly asked suddenly, realizing she hadn't seen her sister in some time. Her mother had said something vague about Eliza still being asleep in the tent. Now Polly began to be alarmed. It wasn't like her sister to be so long away from them. Struggling to her feet, she ran back to the tent, fighting her way through brambles that caught at her skirt and bare feet.

Arriving at the tent, she stopped in horror. Her sister was half-raised on one elbow, trying to call out, her voice hoarse, her face beginning to show the tell-tale purple spots, her whole body shaking.

Polly shouted, calling for help, calling for her parents. No one stirred in the other tents. She shouted again, torn between running for help and staying with her sister. To her relief her father, William, came running having heard the cries. Wordlessly, he gathered Eliza up in his arms and ran towards the newly-constructed hospital. Already it was full. A single bed had just come free, its previous occupant taken away for burial. No question of changing the sheets; there were none to spare.

All that night Polly stayed by her sister, too numb to think or pray, fetching water when her sister cried out, refusing to leave when a nurse finally came by to persuade her to go for her own safety.

The memory of the story of Fionnuala came drifting unbidden into Polly's mind. The story Eliza had told her just as she had heard it. Fionnuala, the sorrowful daughter of Lir, and her three brothers, whose features had so frightened each other as they returned to human form after nine hundred long years ... nine hundred long years.

For Eliza it had just been thirty-one days. Half-crazed with lack of sleep, Polly dozed off, her dreams filled with the white wings of flying swans and the sound of humans moaning all around her.

She woke with a start, frightened by the pressure on her shoulder of a hand that tried to be gentle. It was the harried young nurse, who stood there pointing wordlessly towards the open door of the makeshift hospital.

Panic-stricken, Polly saw that Eliza's bed was empty. "She's gone, run into the bushes like so many of them. I expect you'll find her there," was all the nurse said as she turned, in her own exhaustion, to the next patient.

Polly ran, ran as fast as her trembling legs could carry her. She found herself on the edge of a tiny copse of birch trees. Standing there was a tall man with kind eyes, and broad shoulders that bent a little now. "Was this your sister?" he asked. "The nurse called me. We found her here, face downward in the warm earth." Polly was stunned. Face downwards, like the grief-stricken Scottish princesses of old. Eliza had known the story, had told it in the warm safety of their grandmother's home, had told it to comfort her little sister on a dark night in a strange bed, away from home.

"The soldiers have taken her away already," the tall man said gently. "They have to do that, you know, as quickly as possible, to prevent the spread of the fever."

He understood her next question even before she asked it. "Could you possibly think of this place as her grave?" Even after all the days and nights he had spent on this island, he could still hardly bear the sight of the huge reeking mass graves that held the coffins of the hastily buried dead.

Time slowed down as they stood there. All around them the birch trees were shimmering in the early morning light. Polly remembered the tiny birch grove on the edge of Dromore and Eliza's laughter. It seemed to her the golden light, the light that shines on in the darkness, was all about her now, surrounding her. And, just for a moment, she herself was on the edge of another country, where death had no power, so close she could almost blow away into it.

Sharing the journey.

CHAPTER XX

Grosse-Île Remembered, June 1847

The next day Polly discovered from one of the other families in the tent city that the tall man who had brought her back to her mother was George Mountain, the Anglican Bishop of Montreal, a strong man who had walked the length and breadth of his huge diocese on foot. He had preached in the open air the Sunday before the *Sesostris* arrived. He wrote later in his diary:

Extreme beauty of the day. Preached on part of Psalm 107, its peculiar appropriateness.

> *He hath redeemed them and gathered them*
> *Out of the lands, from the east and the west,*
> *From the north and the south;*
> *They wandered in the wilderness in a solitary way*
> *They found no city to dwell in,*
> *Hungry and thirsty their soul fainted in them,*

Then they cried onto the Lord in their trouble

And he delivered them out of their distresses

And he led them forth by the right way

That they might go to a city of habitation

They that go down to the sea in ships ...

His diary continued: *Chose spot in corner of field, under birch trees affording shade to all. Whole body of worshippers knelt upon the grass. First time officially in open air; mill, barn, school, house, prison, private home, borrowed meeting-home, deck of ships, packets, merchant vessels, steamers, schooners (officiated before).*

One of the moving descriptions that came out of this time was from twenty-six-year-old Bernard McGauran. Barely a year out of his studies, he had been put in charge of the Catholic mission at the island.

Fr. McGauran wrote on May 24, *We have at present thirty-two of these vessels, which are like floating hospitals where death makes the most frightful inroads, and the sick are crowded in among the more healthy. Today I spent five hours in the hold where I administered the sacraments to a hundred people. It would be better to spend one's entire life in a hospital than to spend just a few hours in the hold of one of these vessels ... we meet people everywhere in need of the sacraments; they are dying on the rocks and on the beach where they have been cast by the sailors who simply could not carry them to the hospitals ... I ought to tell your Grace that I am not at all afraid of the fever. I have never felt happier than in my actual state. The Master whom I serve holds me in His all powerful hand.* And then he added, *my legs are beginning to bother me, because I am always on my feet.* Within the month, Bernard McGauran came down with typhus, recovered, and was the last of the priests to leave the island before the navigation season ended.

Within a short time, Polly's family, with others released from quarantine, were brought upstream to Quebec City where kind families took in many of the orphaned children. She marveled at the great fortress walls as they approached, the citadel high above them, the colourful bustle of the Lower Town.

They were taken to a convent where nuns took charge of the children and produced food. Polly and her mother fell into an exhausted sleep, while William prowled restlessly around the port, looking for the steamer that would take them to Montreal.

Emigration Vessel — Between Decks.
Engraving from the Illustrated London News. *May 10, 1851.*

Between Decks. Engraving from the Illustrated London News.

CHAPTER XXI

Montreal, 1847-1850

At last the steamer chugged away from Quebec City's Lower Town pier, its decks so crowded with passengers and baggage that no one could move. The small vessel battled its way against the powerful current of water pouring down from the Great Lakes, and five rivers converging into the St. Lawrence. Tumbling along on its turbulent way, the river had carved out the towering granite bedrock along its shores, swept pebble beaches and dramatic sand dunes into existence and given birth to a teeming multitude of plants, fish, small animals and colourful birds.

Young Joseph was speechless for once when he spotted the shape of a strange fish, larger than he had ever seen in a river in his life. Who had ever heard of a whale in a river? And yet there it was, and there was another. Minke whales, a deckhand told him.

Later in the afternoon William chatted to the pilot as he held the vessel on course past clusters of small islands. The man told him he had counted three hundred and fifty different kinds of birds over the years. A friend of his, an amateur botanist, had collected twelve hundred different kinds of plants and flowers along the banks. "I wouldn't miss working on this river, for all the money in the world," the pilot said. "It's probably the largest body of fresh water globally, if you count the Great Lakes and all the rivers pouring into it. And Montreal where you are going is a fascinating place to live with its location between a mountain and a river. It's becoming one of the largest inland ports worldwide. But stay well away from those fever sheds they've set up. It's tragic what's happening here. People who survived everything else dying in droves, orphaned children still looking for their parents."

William and Jane would never forget the kindliness of the Grey Nuns who welcomed them when they arrived in Montreal and helped them make their way to the home of the Verner family where they were to stay. The Verners were distant relatives who had come out from Ulster seven years before and had written urging all their family in Ireland to come as well. They insisted the Flemings stay with them until they established themselves.

William accepted gratefully. Under no circumstances would he expose Jane and the children to the hardships of a Canadian winter on an isolated farm, even though there were tracts of land on offer. He had no son old enough to help him clear the land of rocks and primaeval forest, as so many had done. His dream of his own farm was put on hold.

That autumn, Polly found herself reluctantly cooped up in a new school, much larger and stricter than the one at home. However, that winter she discovered the joys of skating, sledding and riding through the streets in a horse-drawn sleigh, bells jingling and the smell of wood-smoke filling the air. Everything seemed larger than at home: the moon, the mountain, the pine trees, and the river. Even the sky and the clouds seemed further away, except in the middle of a snow-storm.

Over the next two years, Jane found her health and energy returning. She was still haunted by the stories they heard of the fever sheds, where the mayor of Montreal had also caught the fever and had died of it. All she could do now, however, was concentrate on the fact that she and her husband and half of their children had survived when many had not. Like many of the survivors, she closed a door on the past. She and Polly never spoke again of the Atlantic crossing or Grosse-Île. A new life was ahead of them.

One brisk November evening in 1849, the Verners and Flemings were invited to the nearby home of their friends the Breadons. Alfred Perry, the Captain of the Hook, Ladder & Hose section of the Montreal Fire Brigade had been invited to explain what really happened on that historic night in April when Polly and John had watched the Parliament Building burn to the ground. They already knew the background. All the papers had been full of it. The English population of Montreal, enraged by actions of the colonial government, especially the passage of the Rebellion Losses Bill which gave money to both loyalist and rebels for property losses during the Rebellion of 1837-38, had thronged the streets near the Parliament.

When Polly and her family reached their neighbour's place, warm with a coal fire in the grate, they headed for an empty bench in a room already chock-a-block with English Montrealers.

Alfred Perry began with a picture of St. James and McGill Streets nearly choked with crowds. "Along comes a horse-drawn cab with a furious Tory clinging to the top for dear life, flourishing a bell taken from Dolly's Chop House and shouting at the top of his lungs, 'To the Champ de Mars!' As the Governor-General, Lord Elgin, departs from Parliament, having signed the bill into law, his carriage is pelted with eggs."

Alfred continued, "I was part of a group trying to force our way into the parliamentary chamber. Within a few minutes we were using our thirty-five-foot ladder as a battering ram.

"Inside the chamber, where members were in session, all was confusion. Stones and brickbats from the crowd outside were still coming into the House from all directions. I picked up a brickbat from the floor and let fly at the clock above the Speaker's Chair, its hands showing 9:40. On my third shot I struck the gaselier. Several jets were knocked out. Once the burners were displaced, the gas continued to burn, melting the tubes while the fire gradually kept running up to the ceiling and disappeared burning into the loft.

"The people cheered as I made my way out of the building holding the mace in my hands. I was soon in the street, and, jumping into a calèche, I moved off up to McGill Street, the crowd following, while cheer after cheer broke out from the surging mass, as it reached the corner of St. James Street.

"Meantime the fire had spread to the Hôtel Dieu Nunnery opposite the Parliament building, and its hospital. The fire bells pealed the alarm and the people were in a temper, which begets a panic if the flames were not arrested. The Union fire engine was taken out, and drawn toward the burning Hôtel Dieu when the front wheel dropped off. The nut had been removed from the hub.

"The firemen fought the fire inch by inch until they beat it back to its original centre in the Parliament building. The surrounding buildings had been drenched with water, but not one drop had been thrown on the burning House. Nor would it have been safe for anyone to attempt it.

"At twelve o'clock the fire was over and the bugle had sounded for the troops to fall in; the mob had dispersed and the firemen had packed up and returned to their stations. It was now past one o'clock, and drenched and fatigued I left the scene, accompanied by a few friends. The police arrived shortly after and I was arrested. At the gaol, there was whiskey galore. Although I did not drink I was able to smuggle two quarts to the women prisoners upstairs by dipping the garters which they let down through the ceiling into the stuff. Shortly thereafter I was released through the intervention of the Rev. Dr. Matheson and the senior members of St. Andrews church who arrived en masse at the prison."

Polly and John agreed, as they walked home through the quiet streets, that this was one of the most interesting stories they had ever heard.

By the Don river, Toronto.

The North East Corner of King and Bay Streets. 1850.

CHAPTER XXII

Toronto, 1850

William and Jane were intrigued by the fact that a number of prominent English-speaking Montrealers, among them the Molsons, had signed a petition supporting annexation to the United States. Their own thoughts were, however, turned elsewhere. In the spring of 1850, as soon as navigation on the St. Lawrence commenced again, they packed the family with their few belongings once again onto a steamer, this time bound for Toronto. Jane's younger brother, John Cauldwell, and his wife Margaret, were waiting for them.

As the steamer pulled into Toronto Harbour, Polly caught sight of the Gooderham windmill, its enormous wooden arms revolving steadily in the afternoon breeze. It was an exuberant, welcoming sight, an omen that would set the tone for the eventful years to come. Near the wharf where they disembarked from the steamer was the fish market, thronged with buyers and sellers and their horses and carts. And just leaving the next pier was the horse-driven ferry on its way to the peninsula where a lighthouse stood guard.

With John and Margaret's help, William was able to settle his family in a small house in the downtown area on Stanley Street.[9] He had earned enough money as a carter in Montreal for the first three month's rent and soon obtained his license as one of sixty Toronto carters. By law, when all the church bells started ringing at once to signal a building on fire, every carter had to stop what he was doing and race for the harbour to fetch water, William kept tins ready at their front door. The horse-drawn fire wagon could not carry enough water to put out the blaze.

People had to watch out as it came careening down the road, bicycles following, bugles blowing, volunteer firemen hanging on for dear life. The first carter to arrive at the scene won a prize. William found himself in many an exciting race through the bumpy, pot-holed streets of the darkened city, lit only by one hundred scattered gaslights.

[9] *Now Lombard*

Jane discovered that the house next to theirs was empty and could be rented cheaply. It was a proud day when the new city directory carried the name, Jane Fleming huckster, at 16 Stanley Street. She was in business. Soon she had hens clucking around the yard, had discovered farms where she could buy or barter fruit and vegetables cheaply, and had booked a huckster stall at the new St. Lawrence Market, in a section set aside by a city by-law.

Polly was in her element picking strawberries and gooseberries out in the surrounding fields, with the children in tow. Some of the berries they sold at the market stall, the rest were made into jam, in stone jars just as they had done at home, sealed with goose grease.

Meantime young Joseph rode beside his father as the cart trundled along a narrow path into the primeval forest surrounding St. James Cemetery. From there they brought back wood to sell either at the market stall or door-to-door to the wealthy families on Jarvis Street. Joseph was well able to handle the team himself while his father split wood and talked to his customers. Soon William had enough money to buy a cow so that the children could have fresh milk, and Jane could make butter once again. Every once in a while, as a great treat, the whole family climbed onto Mr. Williams' ten-passenger omnibus that went every hour from the St. Lawrence Market up to the Red Lion Inn on Yonge Street, where all the farmers congregated, in the little village of Yorkville.

A few years later, Jane arranged for all her children to ride with her on the very first horse-drawn street car. This impressive machine trundled off and then came to an abrupt halt, having come off its track. Nothing daunted, the passengers climbed off, gave the thing a push and climbed back on. The excursion was declared a great success by all aboard.

That same year, William had big news for his family — at long last he was able to lease farming land, not far from the Don River, and near the "Don Gaol a-building," as the street directory described it. There he could raise pigs and cows. Soon he had enough money to buy the house at 6 St. David Street, just off Parliament Street, then a main thoroughfare, and near the Park School where his children could get an education.

To their great joy, Jane had given birth to a daughter, Elizabeth, and in 1854 to a son, Robert John, named after the little boy lost at sea, and his great-grandfather John. That year was also an eventful one for Polly, now aged seventeen.

In March, her friend from Montreal, young John Verner had come up to nearby Bolton to visit his Verner cousins, now prosperous farmers. He had arrived at 16 Stanley Street to pay his respects, carrying a ninety-pound bag of oats on his shoulder as though it were full of feathers. On his way out the door to the mill, he had stopped for a moment and whispered in Polly's ear, "Wait for me."

"Wait for what?" she had blurted out in astonishment. After a brief courtship, they were married on May 15 from her parents' home, and moved into their own home on West Charles Street. John could fix anything. He was a licensed tailor, and quite soon he found a good job at the Customs House on the waterfront. When the American Civil War began in 1861, there was huge demand for

Canadian goods from the northern states. John and his colleagues were kept busy with the constant traffic in the harbour. In between, he made sure his wife and her sisters had a lovely dress to wear for special occasions.

To William's great disappointment, his son R. J. left the Park School at age twelve to get a job at $2 a week as stoker in a coal and wood business just around the corner on Parliament Street.

Polly was more than a little worried about this younger brother of hers. He had energy to burn, and was involved in every street fight going.

However, she was coping with dramatic changes in her own life. Over the border in the United States, secret cells of young Irish nationalists, known as Fenians, were meeting in all the major cities. Their audacious plan was to seize Canada, and establish there "A Dominion of the Brotherhood north of the St. Lawrence." On the night of June 1, 1866, an intrepid former Union cavalryman from Kentucky, John O'Neill, took command of two thousand Irish fighting men, crossed the Niagara River and seized Fort Erie, Ontario.

Polly's husband, John, was awakened in the middle of the night and dispatched with his No. 1 Rifle Company to Ridgeway, with too few blankets, and not enough food or supplies. To make matters worse they were given the wrong command to form up. John was then given the signal to take aim at O'Neill. His gun misfired, to Polly's great relief when she heard about it later. A pity if her husband had been responsible for the death of a proud son of

Tyrone. Seven of John's comrades were killed, and their company retreated, as did the Fenians shortly after.

If Canadians had any lingering doubts about the wisdom of climbing down from their proud provincial pedestals to form a new country, the Fenian Raid just about settled the matter. Besides there was an irresistible triumvirate of persuaders at work. Thomas D'Arcy McGee was a silver-tongued, Dublin-bred orator who had once used his gifts on behalf of the Young Irelanders fighting for independence. Jane was fascinated to discover that young McGee had been smuggled off the Inishowen coast of Ireland disguised as a priest when he was being hotly pursued by the authorities. His rescuer was none other than Bishop Maginn of Derry. Jane had known the bishop's mother, Mary Slevin, in Dromore. She was just as well read and just as clever as her brothers, the Slevin schoolmasters, although she had no degree.

"Life is strange," Jane remarked to her family when she came across all this history. "If Mary Slevin had not married a Maginn and given birth to the Bishop, we might not have a country called Canada." But of course there was also the canny lawyer from Kingston, John A. MacDonald, down there wooing Prince Edward Islanders with lobster and champagne. The third man in this powerful triumvirate was George Brown, the feisty editor of the *Toronto Globe.* The result of their efforts was a Confederation celebration on July 1ˢᵗ, 1867, unlike anything Polly and her family had ever witnessed. No one went to bed that night. There was dancing in the streets, just like the nights at home when people danced at the crossroads, fireworks in the sky, and all the church bells ringing.

John lost his job at the Customs House, partly as a result of his absence at Ridgeway, and a decline in trade. Nothing daunted, he and Polly decided to start a small grocery store. A vacant lot was available on Parliament Street, just around the corner from her parents and her brother Joseph. William loaned them the money to buy it. Polly and John scrounged joists and cheap lumber from the yards, and built their own house starting from the back, with a privy (a two-holer), a driving shed for a cart, horse, and winter sleigh, and a shed for a cow. William provided the cow.

This Cabbagetown Store provided the necessities of life on credit to working-class families living on the brink of insolvency, as the larger stores did not. You could buy fresh butter from the big wooden tub, tea mixed with flair by John Verner, juicy red apples from the orchard behind the store, cheap oysters from a barrel at the door of the store and Polly's home-baked pies and cakes. Out of necessity, she had at last learned to cook. Her twin sisters were in and out of the store most days, and when their mother Jane died, they came to live with Polly and John.

Jane, just sixty, died quite suddenly of what the doctor called apoplexy, brought on by exhaustion. She had given birth to eleven children, the last of them a little girl called Maggie who lived for only six years. And she had seen her family established in a new life.

R. J., Polly's brother, was just seventeen when he lost his mother. By his own account later he was "a teenage scrapper who could lick any kid on the block and was headed for serious trouble."

If you were looking for trouble, it wasn't hard to find. The Tecumseh Wigwam Tavern had just been built in 1858 on the northwest corner of Avenue Road and Bloor, not far from Mr. Bloor's brewery, and it was a hangout for all sorts of wild characters. The son of the owner was later hanged publicly at the Gaol for holding up a stagecoach.

R. J. too came to live at the Cabbagetown Store. Under Polly's gentle but firm guidance, he found friends at the Methodist Church on Richmond Street. Soon he was teaching Sunday School there, and became a partner in a coal and wood, flour and feed business on Parliament Street. The next years in his and Polly's lives are a whole other story, as they say in Ireland.*

Tecumseh Wigwam Tavern, at the corner of Avenue Road and Bloor, Toronto.

---

*A glimpse can be found through the website of the Cabbagetown Regent Park Museum. (www.crpmuseum.com). There you can download a free copy of the book Cabbagetown Store by Vern McAree.

See also www.pollyofbridgewaterfarm.com

CHAPTER XXIII

The People's Bob, 1891-1897

On December 14 1891, John Verner showed Polly a banner headline in *The Toronto Telegram*, "Look what your brother is up to now!"

OLD TIME ELECTION CROWD AT CITY HALL

underneath it the text read in part:

Never in the civic history of Toronto was there such a meeting as that held in the City Hall yesterday. It was nomination day. And in view of the vital issues at stake the building was closely packed from floor to ceiling with enthusiastic citizens. It was a field day with a vengeance, and those who for four mortal hours withstood the awful crush will not soon forget the ordeal.

As a representative gathering it has never been surpassed in the annals of the city. Everybody was there; and all the clamouring elements met for once on common ground in

R. J. Fleming at the time of his election as Mayor, City of Toronto.

performance of a common duty. The purse-proud gentlemen of commerce rubbed shoulders with the plebeian crowd of idlers, the intellectual artisan mingled with lawyers and ward heelers, and all of them enjoyed the event.

The candidates were at their best ... But, as one of those present significantly remarked — "There is no doubt about it; this is a Fleming crowd, and don't you forget it."

R. J., "The People's Bob" was elected mayor, not once but four times.

In 1896, he was once again re-elected to City Hall. It was inauguration night for his third term as mayor, elected by the largest landslide in the city's short history. Yet again the room was packed, with no space for the newly elected aldermen to take their usual seats on the floor of the chamber. All the pillars were garlanded with flowers. At the back with the other aldermen, stood William P. Hubbard, son of slaves, Toronto's first black alderman. He and his son would become close associates of the new mayor.

A young reporter for the *Toronto Telegram* dutifully wrote down the names of the notables ensconced in the seats usually occupied by the aldermen. Among them he saw a tiny woman sitting serenely next to her husband. Who was she, he wondered? How did she get there? Polly sat there wondering exactly the same thing, as she looked around her at the huge crowd. For a brief moment she thought back on all that had happened, the dozen children who had been given in to her care, some of them no longer alive — but that was a story for another time. Here and now was R. J. standing there in his element on the platform, the teenage rebel who could have got into serious trouble. How proud his grandfather Joseph would have been.

And away out west was his older brother Joseph, now a pioneering farmer in Manitoba. Well did Polly remember young Joseph's escapades as a tinsmith, scaling some of Toronto's tallest steeples, then cajoling his wife to live with him out west. Three of his children had come to live with her and John at the Cabbagetown Store. During those years there might be twelve to fifteen people in that house built for six. No wonder Polly had a few grey hairs. Now that hair was piled in an elegant crown on the top of her head. Never in all the years of struggle, when the store teetered on the edge of bankruptcy, did she ever allow those children to think they were poor. To each of them she whispered, "You're special," as her grandmother had whispered to her long ago. And every once in a while she would take the week's earnings of the store and buy a lovely hat just like she had seen long ago in the tiny shop window in Omagh, so the children would be proud of her.

At the most difficult times, Polly fell back on the comforting words of the Twenty-third Psalm that her mother had so often repeated just as she and Eliza were falling asleep in the big loft at Bridgewater Farm;

> *The Lord is my shepherd, I shall not want,*
> *He maketh me to lie down in green pastures;*
> *He leadeth me beside the still waters,*
> *He restoreth my soul.*
> *Yea, though I walk through the valley of the shadow of death*
> *I will fear no evil.*
> *For thou art with me;*
> *Thy rod and thy staff they comfort me*
> *Surely goodness and mercy will follow me*
> *all the days of my life*
> *And I will dwell in the house of the Lord forever.*

On May 15, 1914, the *Toronto Telegram* reported that "hundreds of people" came by to salute Polly and her husband John Verner on their sixtieth wedding anniversary. Now, thanks to all the people who helped to put together this unknown Irish story, many others will share in the life of Polly of Bridgewater Farm.

1854 ❖ 1914

Mr. and Mrs. John Verner
request the pleasure of your company
on the occasion of the
Sixtieth Anniversary of their Wedding
on Friday afternoon May fifteenth
nineteen hundred and fourteen
from half past three to six o'clock
at their residence
514 St. Clair Avenue cor. of Bathurst Street
Toronto

The sixtieth wedding anniversary invitation; May 15, 1914.

The family on the porch,
St.Clair & Bathurst Streets, Toronto, c 1916
l. to r. Lydia, Reba, Aunt Polly, Stella, R.J.

EPILOGUE

Polly Verner died in 1918. She lived just long enough to see Thomas White become acting Prime Minister while Robert Borden was representing Canada at the Versailles Treaty Conference. Thomas White, who had lived for a year at the Cabbagetown Store, had been born in a log cabin near Bronte, Ontario, son of Polly's cousin. He had worked as a seventeen-year-old clerk at the Store, encouraged in his studies by Polly. Eventually he became wartime Minister of Finance, and a published poet. Polly's niece, Belle Thompson, would become proud owner of Belle's Tea Room at 44 Oak Street in Cabbagetown, where she served the most delicious scones and homemade jams. Belle's brother, Joseph Thompson, would become a popular Speaker of the Ontario Legislature. Both children came to live at the Store when their mother, Polly's sister Isabella, died in childbirth. Their father, Joseph Thompson, was a printer at the *Globe* when George Brown was shot by a disgruntled employee.

* Portrait of Mary Anne Noble Verner ('Aunt Polly')
in her later years.

Mary Anne Noble Verner ('Aunt Polly')
and one of the orphaned children who came to live at the Cabbagetown Store.

Mary Anne Noble Verner (Polly)
at middle age.

About the Author

Catharine McKenty grew up on her grandparents' farm, "Donlands," then eight miles outside the Toronto city limits on Don Mills Road. She went in every day to Bishop Strachan School, where she won scholarships in French and German. After taking a degree in English at Victoria College, University of Toronto, she spent four winters as a volunteer in the mining area of post-war Germany with an international group of young people involved in reconstruction. Later she was Research Editor for *Pace*, a magazine for young people, based in Los Angeles and New York, and linked with the international musical group *Up With People*.

Next came a stint as a speechwriter for the Ontario Minister of Education in Toronto. At that time she met her future husband,

* The Author, age 10, at Donlands Farm, Don Mills Road, Toronto.

author-broadcaster Neil McKenty on the dance floor. They now live in Montreal. Catharine worked at the *Reader's Digest;* and she and her husband co-authored a best-seller on the early days of Laurentian skiing: ***Skiing Legends and the Laurentian Lodge Club.***

In 2002, Catharine set out to find the Fleming family farm in Northern Ireland, where the Corey family welcomed her and shared their knowledge of the old Irish ways. Catharine did much of her research in the Omagh Public Library (***Tyrone Constitution*** 1844-47, and 100th and 150th anniversary editions). The Ulster American Folk Park; the Ulster Folk and Transport Museum and Linen Hall Library, Belfast.

** Catharine Fleming McKenty,
courtesy of The Tyrone Constitution; *Omagh, Ireland; May 27, 2004.*

View of Quebec.

City of Quebec taken from the Harbour.

218

View of the Harbour, Montreal.

Cathedral, Montreal.

219

Falls of Montmorenci, Winter.

St. James Street, Montreal, 1830.

Place Jacques-Cartier, Montreal, 1897.

Fish Market, Toronto.

Gooderham and Worts Distillery, Toronto, artist A. H. Hider, 1896.

222

Horse-drawn sleigh.

The steam engine Toronto *was the first to be built in Ontario, May 16, 1853, by the Ontario, Simcoe and Huron Union Railroad (O.S. & H. R.R), and ran from Toronto to Machell's Corners (Aurora).*

*Marjorie Hutchison, daughter of Elizabeth Fleming Hutchison,
and adopted by 'Aunt Polly'.*

*R. J. Fleming's children. Left to right: Goldie, Stella, Russell, Lloyd, Victoria,
Murray, Evelyn, and baby Agnes; Toronto, 1905.*

Thomas White
(b. Nov. 13, 1866 d. 1955).

Belle Thompson,
daughter of Isabella Fleming
Thompson and Joseph Thompson.

Agnes and Dr. Evelyn Fleming on either side of Lydia Orford Fleming;
Helen Hyde Fleming (Lloyd Fleming's wife) in India.

R. J. Fleming with his sister,
'Aunt Polly' Verner.

R. J. Fleming's second wife,
Lydia Orford Fleming.

Toronto City Council 1896
with R. J. Fleming standing in front of the mayor's chair.

John Verner (1832-1914).

*Family photo of 'Aunt Polly' Verner
(1837-1918).*

*Toronto City Council 1896 (continued from opposite page)
William Peyton Hubbard, Ward 4, Toronto's first black alderman, seated top right.*

Formal portrait of 'Aunt Polly' and John Verner
on the occasion of their sixtieth wedding anniversary, May 15, 1914.

Family gathering on the occasion of the sixtieth wedding anniversary celebration.

A newspaper article about the event, May 15, 1914.

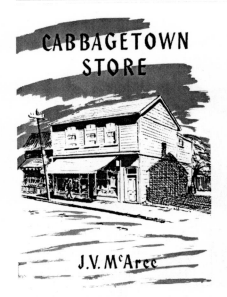

Cover of Vern McAree's book,
Cabbagetown Store.

Portrait of Vern McAree.

A Fleming family dinner at Aunt Polly's home on Bathurst Street,
with Vern McAree standing, back left.

'Aunt Polly' (Mary Anne Noble Verner)
portrait on the occasion of her sixtieth wedding anniversary, May 15, 1914.

"She was, perhaps, the wisest person we ever knew"
Vern McAree
author of **Cabbagetown Store**
www.crpmuseum.com

Horse-drawn Sherbourne streetcar, Toronto.

General View of the City of Toronto, U.C.; ca. 1835
Gooderham Windmill far right.

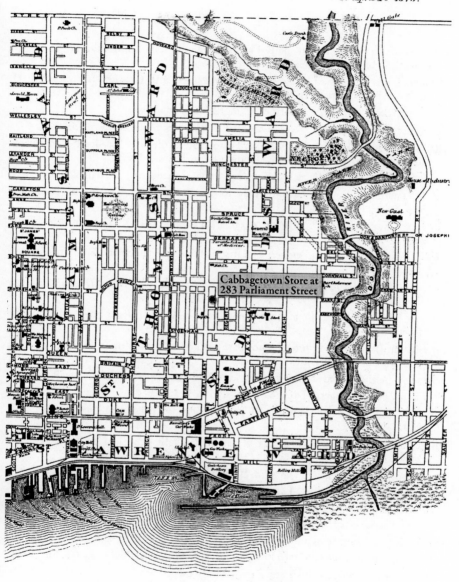

Revised by H.J.& W.A.BROWNE P.L.S.Ton
To April 1st 1878.

Cabbagetown Store at
283 Parliament Street

City of Toronto Map; to April 1, 1878.

Bibliography

1847 Grosse Île; A Record of Daily Events; by André Charbonneau; André Sévigny; Canadian Heritage Parks Canada, 1997

A Paper Landscape; The Ordnance Survey in Nineteenth-Century Ireland; by J. H. Andrews; Four Courts Press, 1993

A Tour in Ireland 1776-1779; by Arthur Young; 2 vol., Dublin

Account of a sea-voyage from Derry to America 1818; Ulster Folk Life Vol. 35, 1989

Against All Odds; The Story of William Peyton Hubbard; Black Leader and Municipal reformer; by Stephen L. Hubbard; Dundurn Press, Toronto, 1987

Around Trillick Way; by Michael McCaughey; Donegal Democrat Ltd., Ballyshannon, 1990

Autobiography of a Country Parson; by the Rev. James Reid Dill MA; Moyola Books and Braid Books, 1996

Christine Kinealy; This Great Calamity; The Irish Famine 1845-52; Gill and MacMillian; Dublin, 1994

Colm Tóibín and Diarmuid Ferriter; The Irish Famine a documentary; St. Martin's Press, New York.

Eyewitness Grosse Île 1847; by Marianna O'Gallagher and Rose Masson Dompierre; Livres Carraig Books, 1995

Farming Life in Ulster; by Jonathan Bell and Mervyn Watson; Ulster Folk and Transport Museum.

Fermanagh, Land of Lake and Legend; Paintings by Frances Morris; Stories by Breege McCusker; Cottage Press.

Folktales of Ireland; Edited and translated by Sean O'Sullivan; University of Chicago Press, 1966

Griffith's Valuation; Pigott's Directory; (Omagh)

Grosse Île; Gateway to Canada, 1832-1937; by Marianna O'Gallagher; Livres Carraig Books, 1984

Images of Omagh, Vols. I-XI; by Dr. Haldane Mitchell; Published by Rotary Club of Omagh.

In Praise of Ulster; by Richard Hayward; William Mullan & Son, Belfast, 1938

Ireland: A Social, Cultural and Literary History, 1791-1891; by James Murphy; Four Courts Press

Irish Folk Ways; Dover Publications Inc.; Mineola, New York, 1957

Irish Lives; by Bernard Shore and William Bolger; Cahill & Co. Ltd.; Dublin, 1971

Irish Passenger Lists, 1847-1871; by Brian Mitchell; Geneological Publishing Co. Inc., 1988

Lowtherstown Workhouse; by Breege McCusker; Necarne Press.

Mayors of Toronto, Volume 1, 1834-1899; Victor L. Russell; The Boston Mills Press.

Not a One-Horse Town; 125 Years of Toronto and its Streetcars; by Mike Filey; printed by Gagne Printing, Louisville, Québec.

Old Dromore; by Patrick Gallagher; Donegal Democrat Ltd.; Ballyshannon

Out of the Past; Ulster Voices Speak; by M. K. Lyle; Vantage Press, 1981

Reminiscences of Charles Durand of Toronto; Barrister; 1897

Siege City: The Story of Derry and Londonderry; by Brian Lacy; Blackstaff Press; Belfast, 1996

Sir William Hingston, 1829-1907; Montreal Mayor, Surgeon and Banker; by Alan Hustak; Price-Patterson; Montreal, 2004 (*ref. pages 34-35 for burning of Parliament house and rescue of the mace.)

Sketches in Dublin and the North; by John Gamble; 1810

St. George and Dill; A study of Two Dromore Clergymen; by Pat McDonnell; Clogher Record, 1989

Statistical Survey of Co. Tyrone; by John McEvoy; Dublin, 1802

The Celtic Realms: History and Culture of the Celtic People; by Myles Dillon and Nora Chadwick; Castle Books; Edison, NJ, 2003

The Famine in Ulster; ed. by Christine Kinealy & Trevor Parkshell; Ulster Historical Foundation; Belfast, 1997

The Fourth Column, J. V. McAree; The MacMillan Company of Canada; 1934

The Irish: A Photohistory; by Sean Sexton & Christine Kinealy; Thames & Hudson; 2002

The Irish Encyclopaedia; ed. by Brian Lalor; foreword by Frank McCourt; Yale University Press; 2003

The Irish Famine — an illustrated history by Helen Litton, 2nd edition 2003 Wolfhound Press

The Maiden City and The Western Ocean; by Sholto Cooke; Morris and Company; Dublin; courtesy Annesley Malley

The Millers and The Mills of Ireland; of about 1850; compiled by William E. Hogg; Sandy Cove, County Dublin, 1997

The Night of the Big Wind; by Peter Carr; The White Row Press; 1991

The Painters Of Ireland c. 1660-1920; By Anne Crookshank and The Knight of Glin; Barrie & Jenkins, London.

The Year in Ireland; A Calendar; by Kevin Danaher; The Mercier Press; Cork, 1972

The Yellow Briar; by Patrick Slater; MacMillan School Edition; 1941

Topographical Dictionary of Ireland; 2 vol.; by Samuel Lewis; London, 1837

Toronto Called Back from 1892-1847; by Conyngham Crawford Taylor; William Briggs; Toronto, 1891

Toronto of Old; Henry Scadding, 1873; Oxford University Press (Canadian Branch); 1966

Toronto Sketches: 'The Way We Were'; by Mike Filey; Dundurn Press; 1992

Voices in Ireland; by P. J. Kavanagh.

Ways of Old Traditional Life in Ireland; by Olive Sharkey; The O'Brien Press; Dublin.

Women of Ireland Image and Experience; c 1880-1920; by Myrtle Hill and Vivienne Pollock; Blackstaff Press; 1993

Glossary

banshee: a female spirit whose wailing warns of a death in a house.

bog: wet spongy ground, consisting chiefly of decayed or decaying moss, peat and other vegetable matter.

brae: steep bank or hillside.

brickbat: a piece of brick, especially when used as a missile.

britches: variation of breeches, meaning trousers, especially fastened below the knee.

can of porridge: cylindrical container made of tin, often with a handle at the top.

carbuncle gem: a name variously applied to precious stones of a red or fiery colour. In the Middle Ages and later besides being a name for the ruby, the term was especially applied to a mythical gem said to emit a light in the dark.

chandler: dealer in candles, oil, soap, paint, groceries, etc.

chilblain: a painful itching swelling of the skin on a hand, foot, etc., caused by exposure to cold and by poor circulation.

churn: vessel or machine for making butter, in which cream or milk is shaken, beaten and broken.

clamp: a heap of potatoes or other root vegetables stored under straw or earth; a pile of turf or peat or garden rubbish etc.

Cooper: a craftsman who makes and repairs wooden vessels formed of staves and hoops, such as casks, buckets, tubs.

creel: a large wicker basket.

delirium tremens: a psychosis of chronic alcoholism involving tremors and hallucinations.

delph: also *delft:* A kind of glazed earthenware made at Delf or Delft in Holland. Originally called Delf ware.

dolmen: or *cromlech:* a megalithic tomb with a large flat stone laid on upright ones.

draper: a retailer of textile fabrics.

drugget: a coarse woven fabric often used for skirts.

drumlin: low, oval mound of compacted boulder clay, moulded by past glacial action.

Fenians: a militant Irish-American society organized in New York in 1859 for the purpose of promoting Irish independence.

firkin: a small cask for liquids, fish, butter etc., with the holding capacity of a quarter of a barrel.

flax: a blue-flowered plant, cultivated for its textile fibre and its seeds, commonly known as linseed. A flax dam is created when many bundles of flax are steeped in water simultaneously in a process called retting, which helps prepare the flax for separation.

frieze: coarse woollen cloth with a nap, usually on one side only.

gout: a disease with inflammation of the smaller joints, esp. the toe, as a result of the deposition of uric acid crystals in the joints.

The Grey Nuns: Catholic congregation of nuns founded in Montreal by Mère d'Youville in 1755. They wear a grey habit and are dedicated to social service.

haggard: a stack yard or area for stacking hay.

harrowing: drawing a harrow over ploughed land. A harrow is a heavy frame with iron teeth used to break up clods of earth, remove weeds, cover seeds, etc.

huckster: a pedlar or hawker, a person who sells or trades in a small way.

incumbent: the holder of an office or post, especially an ecclesiastical benefice; in occupation or having the tenure of a post or position.

lough: a lake or arm of the sea

man-o'-war: or *man-of-war:* an armed ship, especially of a specified country *moile cow:* so called from the Irish word describing the distinctive mound or dome on the top of its head, A hornless breed, it is traditionally a dairy cow, producing fine quality beef and milk from inferior quality grazing.

noggin: a small drinking vessel; a mug or cup.

poke: a bag or a sack.

poteen: alcohol made illicitly, usually from potatoes

privy: a lavatory, often built outside the house (from privé, meaning private, secret).

purdy bread: possibly a variation of purty bread meaning bread made from potatoes.

quarters: a grain measure in Britain equivalent to 8 bushels. A bushel was the equivalent in Britain of 8 gallons or 36.4 litres.

rag nails: similar to **hangnails:** small pieces of skin in the nail area detached from the surrounding skin.

Rapparee: a 17th- century Irish irregular soldier or freebooter; a lawless adventurer (from Irish: *rapaire:* short pike), an infantry weapon with a pointed steel or iron head on a wooden shaft.

reiver: variation of verb to reave, an old-fashioned or archaic word meaning to carry off, take by force, make raids, plunder.

Repeal Year: Irish nationalist leader and social reformer, Daniel O'Connell (1775-1847) worked to annul, or repeal, the Act of Union, which, in 1801 had united England and Ireland under a single Parliament.

ribaldry: coarse or humorously dirty talk or behaviour.

rickle: a heap or pile, especially one loosely built up.

Saint Brighid's cross: named after Saint Brighid or Bridget, a 6th-century Irish abbess, noted in miracle stories for her compassion. The crosses bearing her name are traditionally woven from rushes. Although their shape is seen as a Christian symbol, it may originally derive from the pagan sun-wheel.

scutch: to beat oats, flax etc.

slane: a long-handled spade, having a wing at one or both sides of the blade, used in Ireland for cutting turf.

smoor: to smother, stifle, suffocate; to put out, or extinguish a light or fire.

spade: a tool used for digging or cutting the ground etc., with a sharp-edged metal blade and a long handle

sowing fiddle: also called a seed fiddle: a traditional instrument used to broadcast or disseminate seed. A bag holding seed feeds into a dispenser carried over one shoulder. A bow below it is moved back and forth by the sower's opposite hand, resulting in the seed being sprayed out in a wide arc.

spancel: a rope or fetter for hobbling cattle, horses, etc.; especially a short-noosed rope used for fettering the hind legs of a cow during milking.

sparbled: variant of verb to sparple: to scatter, disperse, send in all directions.

St. Elmo's Fire: luminous electrical discharges seen especially on a ship or aircraft during a storm. St. Elmo, the patron saint of seafarers.

Strule: the river Strule, roughly 26 miles long, runs near the town of Omagh in County Tyrone, Northern Ireland

tallow: the harder kinds of fat, especially animal fat, melted down for use in making candles, soap etc.

temperance: the temperance movement sought restrictions on the consumption of alcohol. Groups with such an aim appeared in the early 19th century, first in New England and Northern Ireland and spread across Europe and the U.S.

tinker: a traveling or itinerant mender of kettles and pans, etc.

yaws: a contagious tropical skin disease characterized by inflamed raspberry-like swellings on the skin.

Sources:

Compact Edition of the Oxford English Dictionary, 1971 (two vols)
Oxford English Reference Dictionary. 1996
Oxford Dictionary of Quotations, 1996
Colombo's Canadian References, OUP, 1976

List of Illustrations

Family photos courtesy of Catharine Fleming McKenty unless otherwise noted;
Inner front cover: **The Catchment Area of Derry for the Emigrant Trade to North America in 1850.** *Courtesy of Annesley Malley, Ireland;*
Inner back cover: **Detail of H. J. Browne's Map of The City of Toronto, 1862.** *City of Toronto Archives MT845;*
Illustrations by Ela and Darek Wieczorek unless otherwise noted;

P. 222 *Upper:* **Fish Market, Toronto;** artist W. H. Bartlett; printer J. C. Bentley; Toronto Public Library; John Ross Robertson Collection; JRR1845

Lower: **Gooderham and Worts Distillery, Toronto,** A. H. Hider, 1896. DHD

P. 223 *Upper:* **Horse drawn sleigh;** winter; W. Weller; watercolour; Toronto Public Library; John Ross Robertson Collection; JRR888

Lower: **The steam engine 'Toronto'** was the first to be built in Ontario, May 16th, 1853, by the Ontario, Simcoe and Huron Union Railroad (O.S. & H. R.R), and ran from Toronto to Machell's Corners (Aurora). Toronto Public Library; John Ross Robertson Collection; JRR1115

P. 224 *Upper:* **Marjorie Hutchison,** daughter of Elizabeth Fleming Hutchison, and adopted by 'Aunt Polly'

Lower: **R. J. Fleming's children.** Left to right: Goldie, Stella, Russell, Lloyd, Victoria, Murray, Evelyn, and baby Agnes; Toronto 1905

P. 225 *Upper left:* **Thomas White** (b. Nov. 13, 1866, d. 1955); Cousin of Aunt Polly. Worked as a reporter for the now discontinued Toronto Evening Star, appointed Finance Minister during the First World War, and served as acting Prime Minister of Canada for Sir Robert Borden

Upper right: **Belle Thompson,** daughter of Isabella Fleming Thompson and Joseph Thompson. Belle became known for the quality of her tea and her hospitality at BELLE'S TEA ROOM, located on the ground floor of her home at 44 Oak Street

Lower: **Agnes and Dr. Evelyn Fleming on either side of Lydia Orford Fleming; Helen Hyde Fleming** (Lloyd Fleming's wife) **in India**

P. 226 *Upper left:* **R. J. Fleming with his sister,** 'Aunt Polly' Verner

Upper right: **R. J. Fleming's second wife,** Lydia Orford Fleming

Lower left: **Toronto City Council 1896** with R. J. Fleming standing in front of the mayor's chair, (part left). Daniel Lamb is seated directly right of R. J.

P. 227 *Upper left:* **John Verner** (1842-1914)

Upper right: **Family photo of 'Aunt Polly' Verner** (1837-1918)

Lower: **Toronto City Council 1896** with R. J. Fleming standing in front of the mayor's chair, (part right). Daniel Lamb is seated directly right of R. J.

P. 228 *Upper:* **Formal portrait of 'Aunt Polly' and John Verner** on the occasion of their sixtieth wedding anniversary, May 15th, 1914

Lower: **Family gathering** on the occasion of the sixtieth wedding anniversary celebration.

P. 229 A newspaper article about the event, May 15th, 1914

P. 230 *Upper left:* **Cover of Vern McAree's book, Cabbagetown Store;** published by Ryerson Press (Toronto, 1953)

Upper right: **Portrait of Vern McAree**

Lower: **A Fleming family dinner at Aunt Polly's home on Bathurst Street,** with Vern McAree standing, back, left

P. 231 **'Aunt Polly' (Mary Anne Noble Verner) portrait** on the occasion of her sixtieth wedding anniversary, May 15th, 1914

P. 232 *Upper:* **Horse-drawn Sherbourne streetcar, Toronto;** Toronto Public Library; TPL 986-18-4

Lower: **General View of the City of Toronto, U.C.;** Thomas Young (artist); N. Currier (printer), ca. 1835; ROM 960X280.8 With the permission of the Royal Ontario Museum © ROM

P. 233 **City of Toronto Map;** revised by H. J. and W. A. Browne, P.L.S.; to April 1st, 1878

To find out more about
POLLY
*and her family's life
in Toronto, Canada
visit the*

CABBAGETOWN REGENT PARK
COMMUNITY MUSEUM

**A not-for-profit
museum representing two
neighbouring communities
passionate about our past
and on-going histories
in a global context.**

http://crpmuseum.com

The museum has a temporary home
at the Riverdale Farm's Residence House.
201 Winchester Street
Toronto, Ontario M4X 1B8
416-392-6794

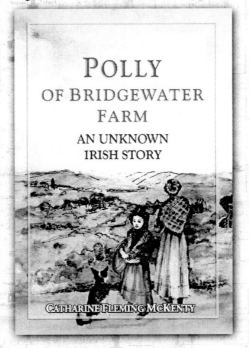

CPSIA information can be obtained at www.ICGtesting.com
Printed in the USA
BVOW04s1941040214

343652BV00007B/218/P